Friedrich Schiller, Theodore Wirgman

Wallenstein's Camp

Friedrich Schiller, Theodore Wirgman

Wallenstein's Camp

ISBN/EAN: 9783337019921

Printed in Europe, USA, Canada, Australia, Japan

Cover: Foto ©Andreas Hilbeck / pixelio.de

More available books at **www.hansebooks.com**

WALLENSTEIN'S CAMP

BY

FREDERICK VON SCHILLER.

TRANSLATED INTO ENGLISH VERSE

BY

THEODORE WIRGMAN, LL. B.

TRINITY - COLLEGE, CAMBRIDGE,

LIEUT. COLONEL ON H. P., LATE 6th INNISKILLING DRAGOONS,

FORMERLY OF THE IMPERIAL AUSTRIAN SERVICE.

——————— ——— ——

LONDON: 1871,

DAVID NUTT, 270, STRAND.

PREFACE.

Two tranlations of Wallenstein's Camp having already appeared — one by the late Earl of Ellesmere, the other by Mr. James Churchill in "Bohn's Standard Library" — this maiden - attempt is with great diffidence offered to the public. A lenient judgment is then expected; especially as it was undertaken to while away the dull hours of a monsoon, which in 1866 broke so heavily over the cantonments of Mhow, East Indies, as to cause a cessation of all, but ordinary, military duties, and to render leisure irksome without some appointed task.

Wallenstein's Camp is a prelude to Schiller's "Piccolomini" and "Wallenstein's Death" and displays, as T. S. Coleridge — the successful translator of those renowned Dramas — says, "a lively picture of laxity of discipline and the mutinous dispositions of Wallenstein's soldiery". He considers that a translation of it "into prose or into any other metre than that of the original would have given a false idea of its style and purport"; a translation "into the same metre would have been incompatible with a faithful adherence to the sense of the German from the comparative poverty of our language in rhymes and it would have been unadvisable, from the incongruity of those lax verses with the present taste of the English public". *(See Preface to Piccolomini.)*

Notwithstanding this opinion it appears that the original is susceptible of a nearly literal translation into English verse without losing much of its spirit and vigour. But to accomplish this, it is requisite to have a thorough knowledge of both languages and also to have an insight into the military customs of the Imperial Austrian Army, which did, till lately, bear marked traces of its descent from the Wallensteiners of the Thirty Years' War.

A ten years' service in the Austrian Cavalry and Staff Corps has given the Translator the opportunity of acquiring both these requisites, which, he trusts, have not been in vain employed.

As few deviations from the original, as possible, have been made; but some were permitted to convey to the Reader in an English form the puns and play upon words, that in German flow so glibly from the tongue of the Capuchin Friar. His humorous address cannot be rendered quite literally; yet it is hoped that the wit, humour, and spirit of the original have not suffered much by having assumed an English garb. Some English slang phrases have here and there been admitted to render the conversations of the soldiery more forcible and adapt them to the tone prevailing in the barrackyard. This offence, however, against refined taste will, no doubt, be pardoned, when it is considered that Schiller represented soldiers such as they were and not such as they ought to be.

The German text is placed opposite to the English to enable the Reader to compare one with the other, and thus to judge more readily of the faithfulness of the Translation.

In conclusion, the Author begs the public to take into consideration that this translation was made in a place, where no assistance could be procured, and at a time, when he was ignorant of any previous attempt; for all faults he, therefore, claims especial indulgence.

United Service Club,
London, February 1871.

T. W.

WALLENSTEIN'S CAMP.

1

Personen.

- - -

Wachtmeister, | von einem Terzky'schen Carabinier = Regiment.
Trompeter, |
Konstabler.
Scharfschützen.
Zwei Holkische reitende Jäger.
Buttlerische Dragoner.
Arkebusiere vom Regiment Tiefenbach.
Kürassier von einem wallonischen | Regiment.
Kürassier von einem lombardischen |
Kroaten.
Uhlanen.
Rekrut.
Bürger.
Bauer.
Bauerknabe.
Kapuziner.
Soldatenschulmeister.
Marketenderin.
Eine Aufwärterin.
Soldatenjungen.
Hoboisten.

Vor der Stadt Pilsen in Böhmen.

———

DRAMATIS PERSONÆ.

Serjeant - Major, } *of one of Count Terzky's Carabinier - Regi-*
Trumpeter,   }   *ments.*
Bombardier, *or* Artilleryman.
Riflemen.
Two Mounted Chasseurs, *of Holk's Corps.*
Dragoons, *of Butler's Regiment.*
Arquebusiers, *of Tiefenbach's Regiment.*
Cuirassier, *of a Walloon Regiment.*
Cuirassier, *of a Lombard Regiment.*
Croats.
Uhlans *or* Polish Lancers.
Recruit. Citizen. Peasant.
Peasant - Boy. Capuchin Friar.
Regimental - Schoolmaster. Cantinière *or* Sutler - Woman.
Sutler's Serving - girl.
Soldier's Boys. Bandsmen.

(Scene — *The Camp before Pilsen in Bohemia.*)

---

1 *

Erster Auftritt.

Marketenderzelte, davor eine Kram= und Trödelbude. Soldaten von allen Farben und Feldzeichen drängen sich durch einander, alle Tische sind besetzt. Kroaten und Uhlanen an einem Kohlfeuer kochen. Marketenderin schenkt Wein, Soldatenjungen würfeln auf einer Trommel, im Zelt wird gesungen.

Ein Bauer und sein Sohn.

Bauerknabe.

Vater, es wird nicht gut ablaufen,
Bleiben wir von dem Soldatenhaufen.
Sind euch gar trotzige Kameraden;
Wenn sie uns nur nichts am Leibe schaden!

Bauer.

Ei was! Sie werden uns ja nicht fressen,
Treiben sie's auch ein wenig vermessen.
Siehst du? sind neue Völker herein,
Kommen frisch von der Saal' und dem Main,
Bringen Beut' mit, die rarsten Sachen!
Unser ist's, wenn wir's nur listig machen.
Ein Hauptmann, den ein andrer erstach,
Ließ mir ein paar glückliche Würfel nach.
Die will ich heut einmal probieren,
Ob sie die alte Kraft noch führen.
Mußt dich nur recht erbärmlich stellen,
Sind gar lockere, leichte Gesellen

Scene I.

Sutlers' tents, — in front a Slop-Shop. — Soldiers in all kinds of uniforms mingling in the crowd. — Tables all filled. — Croats and Uhlans cooking at a coal-fire. — The Cantinière serving out wine. — Soldier-boys throwing dice on a drum-head. — Then singing is heard from the Tent.

Enter a Peasant and his Son.

Peasant-Boy.

Father! It won't end well; so let us stay
From that dense crowd of soldiers far away.
Tow'rds us they are companions more like roughs;
Oh! that they hurt us not with blows and cuffs!

Peasant.

No matter! They won't eat us, I'll be bound,
Though rough and ready chaps they 're always found.
Look ye! Strange people mingle in the train
Fresh coming from the rivers Saal and Mayn;
They bring both booty rare and choice supplies;
It's ours — if cunning tricks will blind their eyes.
A Captain, whom a comrade pink'd in duel,
Bequeath'd me lucky dice worth any jewel
By Jove! to-day I'll try their pow'r once more,
And see, if they can reach their olden score.
You must a pitiful demeanour feign;
These chaps are loose and dissolute of vein,

Lassen sich gerne schön thun und loben,
So wie gewonnen, so ist's zerstoben.
Nehmen sie uns das Unsre in Scheffeln,
Müssen wir's wieder bekommen in Löffeln;
Schlagen sie grob mit dem Schwerte drein,
So sind wir pfiffig und treiben's fein.

(Im Zelt wird gesungen und gejubelt.)

Wie sie juchzen — daß Gott erbarm!
Alles das geht von des Bauern Felle.
Schon acht Monate legt sich der Schwarm
Uns in die Betten und in die Ställe,
Weit herum ist in der ganzen Aue
Keine Feder mehr, keine Klaue,
Daß wir für Hunger und Elend schier
Nagen müssen die eigenen Knochen.
War's doch nicht ärger und krauser hier,
Als der Sachs noch im Lande thät pochen.
Und die nennen sich Kaiserliche —

Bauerknabe.

Vater, da kommen ein paar aus der Küche,
Sehen nicht aus, als wär' viel zu nehmen.

Bauer.

Sind einheimische, geborne Böhmen,
Von des Terschkas Karabinieren,
Liegen schon lang in diesen Quartieren.
Unter allen die schlimmsten just,
Spreizen sich, werfen sich in die Brust,
Thun, als wenn sie zu fürnehm wären,
Mit dem Bauer ein Glas zu leeren.
Aber dort seh' ich die drei scharfe Schützen
Linker Hand um ein Feuer sitzen,

Fond of *soft solder*, and delight in praise;
"Light come, light go" — the proverb wisely says.
By bushels they our goods and chattels take,
Which we by driblets good again must make;
They on brute force with sword in hand rely,
Whilst we to craft and cunning e'er must fly.

(Singing and hurrahs in the tent.)

Oh! Lord have mercy on them all! What shouts!
All that comes from the hides of country-louts.
With leave or not, this horde — for eight months past —
Lies in our beds and holds our stables fast.
No game in woods, no fowl in farms around,
No creeping thing can here for food be found;
To still our hunger in this dearth unknown,
We have to gnaw our flesh clean off the bone.
Things were not worse, nor scourg'd a fiercer hand,
When Saxons wild o'erran our Fatherland;
And they th'Imperial badge presume to wear. —

Peasant-Boy.

Father! from cook-house come two fellows here,
Such ragamuffins can't of much be shorn.

Peasant.

They're natives of this land, Bohemians born,
To Terzky's Carabiniers they both belong,
And hereabouts have lain in quarters long.
Conceited apes! They're worse than all the rest.
How proud they strut about, throw out the chest,
And noble airs affect, as if too grand
To drink a glass with us, who till the land.
I see three Riflemen in gay attire
There sitting on your left around a fire,

Sehen mir aus wie Tyroler schier.
Emmerich komm! an die wollen wir,
Lustige Vögel, die gerne schwatzen,
Tragen sich sauber und führen Batzen.

(Gehen nach den Zelten.)

Zweiter Auftritt.

Vorige. Wachtmeister. Trompeter. Uhlan.

Trompeter.

Was will der Bauer da? Fort, Hallunk!

Bauer.

Gnädige Herren, einen Bissen und Trunk!
Haben heut noch nichts Warmes gegessen.

Trompeter.

Ei, das muß immer saufen und fressen.

Uhlan (mit einem Glase).

Nichts gefrühstückt? Da, trink, du Hund!

(Führt den Bauer nach dem Zelte; jene kommen vorwärts.)

Wachtmeister (zum Trompeter).

Meinst du, man hab' uns ohne Grund
Heute die doppelte Löhnung gegeben,
Nur daß wir flott und lustig leben?

Trompeter.

Die Herzogin kommt ja heute herein
Mit dem fürstlichen Fräulein —

Wachtmeister.

Das ist nur der Schein.

Die Truppen, die aus fremden Landen
Sich hier vor Pilsen zusammen fanden,

To me like Tyrolese they all appear.
Come Emmerich! Let us to them draw near,
Jolly birds! how they love a chat! We'll join
Those civil chaps; they always have some coin.

(They move towards the tent.)

Scene II.

The above. — Serjeant - Major, Trumpeter, Uhlan.

Trumpeter.

What want ye here? Go lout! Obey my wink!

Peasant.

Good Sirs! a somewhat just to eat and drink!
As yet I've tasted nothing warm to day.

Trumpeter.

Eating and drinking always — that's your way.

Uhlan (with a glass).

No breakfast yet? Take that, you dog! and drink!

(He leads the Peasant to the tent — the others come forward.)

Serjeant - Major (to the Trumpeter).

Without some solid reason do ye think,
That we this day have got our double pay?
Is it that we should revel, feast and play?

Trumpeter.

The Duchess brings her princely daughter here
To day —

Serjeant - Major.

'T is only moonshine — That's quite clear
The troops, that march'd from countries far away
To join our camp, and here round Pilsen lay,

Die sollen wir gleich an uns locken
Mit gutem Schluck und guten Brocken,
Damit sie sich gleich zufrieden finden
Und fester sich mit uns verbinden.

Trompeter.
Ja, es ist wieder was im Werke.

Wachtmeister.
Die Herrn Generäle und Kommendanten —

Trompeter.
Es ist gar nicht geheuer, wie ich merke.

Wachtmeister.
Die sich so dick hier zusammen fanden —

Trompeter.
Sind nicht für die Langweil herbemüht.

Wachtmeister.
Und das Gemunkel und das Geschicke —

Trompeter.
Ja, Ja!

Wachtmeister.
Und von Wien die alte Perrücke,
Die man seit gestern herumgehn sieht,
Mit der guldenen Gnadenkette,
Das hat was zu bedeuten, ich wette.

Trompeter.
Wieder so ein Spürhund, gebt nur Acht,
Der die Jagd auf den Herzog macht.

Wachtmeister.
Merkst du wohl? Sie trauen uns nicht,
Fürchten des Friedländers heimlich Gesicht.
Er ist ihnen zu hoch gestiegen,
Möchten ihn gern herunterkriegen.

We must decoy and win them o'er to us
By drink, good cheer, and ev'ry sort of fuss,
That they in such good comrades may delight
And then with us firm hand-in-hand unite.

Trumpeter.

At work behind the scenes there's something yet!

Serjeant-Major.

The Gen'rals, Chiefs of Corps and all that set —

Trumpeter.

All is not so secure, as I surmise.

Serjeant-Major.

In crowds flock'd here, then buzz about like flies —

Trumpeter.

They're not come here to drive dull care away.

Serjeant-Major.

Those secret whisp'rings and dispatches rare —

Trumpeter.

Just so!

Serjeant-Major.

      And bigwigs grave from Vienna too,
Who came since yesterday so oft in view,
Deck'd with gold-chains of honour richly set;
There's something in't — a trifle I would bet.

Trumpeter.

I' faith! some bloodhound, bear ye well in mind,
That's put on scent the Duke again to find.

Serjeant-Major.

Mark well! They trust us not — their faith we shook;
They dread our Friedland's all-concealing look.
Too high for them he soar'd in his proud vein,
So they would gladly pull him down again.

Trompeter.

Aber wir halten ihn aufrecht, wir,
Dächten doch alle, wie ich und ihr!

Wachtmeister.

Unser Regiment und die andern vier,
Die der Terschka anführt, des Herzogs Schwager,
Das resoluteste Corps im Lager,
Sind ihm ergeben und gewogen,
Hat er uns selbst doch herangezogen.
Alle Hauptleute setzt' er ein,
Sind alle mit Leib und Leben sein.

Dritter Auftritt.

Kroat mit einem Halsschmuck. Scharfschütze folgt. Vorige.

Scharfschütz.

Kroat, wo hast du das Halsband gestohlen?
Handle dirs ab! dir ist's doch nichts nütz.
Geb dir dafür das Paar Terzerolen.

Kroat.

Nix, nix! Du willst mich betrügen, Schütz.

Scharfschütz.

Nun! geb dir auch noch die blaue Mütz,
Hab sie so eben im Glücksrad gewonnen.
Siehst du? Sie ist zum höchsten Staat.

Kroat.
(läßt das Halsband in der Sonne spielen).

's ist aber von Perlen und edelm Granat.
Schau, wie das flinkert in der Sonnen!

Trumpeter.

But we support him and maintain his might.
Thought all as you and I — it would be right!

Serjeant - Major.

Our Reg'ment and those four — renown'd in deeds —
Which our Duke's Sister's spouse, Count Terzky, leads,
For pluck no corps in camp wins more applause,
Are true and e'er devoted to his cause;
For we by him alone were train'd and led;
Of all our honours he's the fountain-head;
The Captains all from him commissions bear;
To him for life they true allegiance swear.

Scene III.

Enter Croat with a Necklace — Rifleman follows — The above.

Rifleman.

Croat! Where did you that smart necklace steal?
'Tis of no use to you — so make a deal:
I'll give these pocket-pistols in exchange.

Croat.

From me, you Rogue! You want to take the change!

Rifleman.

Come! a blue cap I'll just throw in our deal,
That I this moment won at Fortune's wheel.
Look here! at court 'tis fashion's highest pet!

Croat.

(whirling the Necklace in the sunlight.)

It is with perls and precious garnets set.
Now look! How bright it glitters in the sun!

Scharfschütz (nimmt das Halsband).

Die Feldflasche noch geb' ich drein,

(Besieht es.)

Es ist mir um den schönen Schein.

Trompeter.

Seht nur, wie der den Kroaten prellt!
Halbpart, Schütze, so will ich schweigen.

Kroat (hat die Mütze aufgesetzt).

Deine Mütze mir wohlgefällt.

Scharfschütz (winkt dem Trompeter).

Wir tauschen hier! Die Herrn sind Zeugen!

Vierter Auftritt.

Vorige. Konstabler.

Konstabler (tritt zum Wachtmeister).

Wie ist's, Bruder Karabinier?
Werden wir uns lang noch die Hände wärmen,
Da die Feinde schon frisch im Felde herum schwärmen?

Wachtmeister.

Thut's Ihm so eilig, Herr Konstabel?
Die Wege sind noch nicht praktikabel.

Konstabler.

Mir nicht. Ich sitze gemächlich hier
Aber ein Eilbot' ist angekommen,
Meldet, Regensburg sei genommen.

Trompeter.

Ei, da werden wir bald aufsitzen.

Rifleman (taking the Necklace).

I'll throw my flask in — now the deal is done.

(looks at it.)

I only care about its lustrous shine.

Trumpeter.

Ah! you have stuck that Croat pretty fine!
Go halves, my boy! And sure then I won't peach;
For mum's the word — and silent is my speech.

Croat (having put on the cap).

Your cap doth please me much.

Rifleman (winking at the Trumpeter).

Oh! never fear!
A mere exchange! To that, Sirs, witness bear!

Scene IV.

The above. — A Bombardier (or Artilleryman).

Bombardier (moving towards the Serjeant-Major).

How goes it then? My comrade Carabinier!
Shall we much longer still sit quiet here,
And keep our hands so comfortably warm,
Whilst to the field again our foes fresh swarm?

Serjeant-Major.

But, Bombardier! whatever haste you make,
Impracticable are the roads you'll take.

Bombardier.

Pooh! Pooh! In comfort I will here stick fast;
But now a Courrier, who just gallop'd past,
Reports, that Ratisbon is seiz'd by force.

Trumpeter.

All right! Then soon again we'll take to horse.

Wachtmeister.

Wohl gar, um dem Bayer sein Land zu schützen,
Der dem Fürsten so unfreundlich ist?
Werden uns eben nicht sehr erhitzen.

Konstabler.

Meint ihr? — Was ihr nicht alles wißt!

Fünfter Auftritt.

Vorige. Zwei Jäger. Dann Marketenderin. Soldatenjungen. Schulmeister. Aufwärterin.

Erster Jäger.

Sieh, sieh!

Da treffen wir lustige Compagnie.

Trompeter.

Was für Grünröck mögen das sein?
Treten ganz schmuck und stattlich ein.

Wachtmeister.

Sind Holkische Jäger; die silbernen Tressen
Holten sie sich nicht auf der Leipziger Messen.

Marketenderin (kommt und bringt Wein).

Glück zur Ankunft, ihr Herrn!

Erster Jäger.

Was? der Blitz!

Das ist ja die Gustel aus Blasewitz.

Marketenderin.

I freilich! Und Er ist wohl gar, Mußjö,
Der lange Peter aus Itzehö?
Der seines Vaters goldene Füchse

Serjeant-Major.

What so! — e'en to protect Bavaria's soil?
Whose sons our Prince in ev'ry plan would foil?
Too warm in such a cause we will not grow!

Bombardier.

So you suppose! — What wonders you must know!

Scene V.

*The above. — Two Chasseurs à cheval. — Afterwards Cantinière. — Sol-
diers' Sons. — Schoolmaster. Sutler's serving-girl.*

First Chasseur.

Up now, my lads! Let's join this jolly set!
For boon companions there are always met.

Trumpeter.

Who are those dashing fellows dress'd in green?
Who strut in now with smart and stately mien.

Serjeant-Major.

They're Holk's Chasseurs. The silver lace they wear,
I'll bet, they did not buy at Leipsic-fair.

Cantinière (enters bringing wine).

Sirs! Welcome here!

First Chasseur.

          That beats all into fits!
Why? Sure that's Gussy self from Blasewitz.

Cantinière.

Ay! yes. But I am sure that you, Sir! you
Are lanky Peter self from Itzehö:
Who with our Reg'ment in one jolly night

2

Mit unserm Regiment hat durchgebracht
Zu Glückstadt, in einer lustigen Nacht —

Erster Jäger.
Und die Feder vertauscht mit der Kugelbüchse.

Marketenderin.
Ei, da sind wir alte Bekannte!

Erster Jäger.
Und treffen uns hier im böhmischen Lande.

Marketenderin.
Heute da, Herr Vetter, und morgen dort —
Wie einen der rauhe Kriegesbesen
Fegt und schüttelt von Ort zu Ort;
Bin indeß weit herum gewesen.

Erster Jäger.
Will's Ihr glauben! Das stellt sich dar.

Marketenderin.
Bin hinauf bis nach Temeswar
Gekommen mit den Bagagewagen,
Als wir den Mansfelder thäten jagen.
Lag mit dem Friedländer vor Stralsund,
Ging mir dorten die Wirthschaft zu Grund.
Zog mit dem Succurs vor Mantua,
Kam wieder heraus mit dem Feria,
Und mit einem spanischen Regiment
Hab' ich einen Abstecher gemacht nach Gent.
Jetzt will ich's im böhmischen Land probieren,
Alte Schulden eincassieren —
Ob mir der Fürst hilft zu meinem Geld.
Und das dort ist mein Marketenderzelt.

Erster Jäger.
Nun, da trifft Sie alles beisammen an!

At Glückstadt spent the yellow-boys outright,
Which the poor father hoarded for his son —

First Chasseur.

And thus exchang'd the pen for rifle-gun.

Cantinière.

From years long gone then our acquaintance dates!

First Chasseur.

And meet once more in old Bohemia's states.

Cantinière.

I'm here to-day, and there to-morrow seen —
For War's rough besom sweeps all rubbish clean,
And makes one scuttle quick from place to place;
I've been the world around within an ace.

First Chasseur.

I'm sure you have! one sees that from afar.

Cantinière.

For I have been right down to Temeswar,
Marching with baggage-trains from town to town,
Whilst we Count Mansfeld's corps were hunting down.
I lay in Friedland's camp 'neath Stralsund's wall;
But there I came to grief, and lost my all.
I join'd the succours then to Mantua sent,
With Feria back again I homeward went,
And with a Spanish Reg'ment then I made
A rambling march to Ghent, which never paid.
I now will try Bohemia's mountain-land,
And see what debts will turn to cash-in-hand;
Whether the Prince to aid me is intent.
There yonder 's my canteen — my sutler's tent.

First Chasseurs.

You'll meet there now together all the lot!

2*

Doch wo hat Sie den Schottländer hingethan,
Mit dem Sie damals herumgezogen?

Marketenderin.

Der Spitzbub! Der hat mich schön betrogen.
Fort ist er! Mit allem davon gefahren,
Was ich mir thät am Leibe ersparen.
Ließ mir nichts, als den Schlingel da!

Soldatenjunge (kommt gesprungen).

Mutter! sprichst du von meinem Papa?

Erster Jäger.

Nun, nun, das muß der Kaiser ernähren.
Die Armee sich immer muß neu gebären.

Soldatenschulmeister (kommt).

Fort in die Feldschule! Marsch, ihr Buben!

Erster Jäger.

Das fürcht sich auch vor der engen Stuben!

Aufwärterin (kommt).

Base, sie wollen fort.

Marketenderin.

Gleich, gleich!

Erster Jäger.

Ei, wer ist denn das kleine Schelmengesichte?

Marketenderin.

's ist meiner Schwester Kind — aus dem Reich.

Erster Jäger.

Ei, also eine liebe Nichte? (Marketenderin geht.)

Zweiter Jäger (das Mädchen haltend).

Bleib Sie bei uns doch, artiges Kind.

Aufwärterin.

Gäste dort zu bedienen sind.

(Macht sich los und geht.)

But prithee! What became of your poor Scot,
With whom you company kept in former days?

Cantinière.

The rogue! The tricks, he play'd, would make you gaze!
Bolted with all! The thief, so ill behav'd,
Stole all my earnings — all that I had sav'd,
And left me nothing but that booby lad!

Soldier-Boy (comes springing forward).

Dost thou, dear Mother! speak of my poor dad?

First Chasseur.

Him must the Kaiser bring up now and feed;
For fresh recruits will Armies always need.

Enter Regimental-Schoolmaster.

Pack off to School, you boys! and be not late!

First Chasseur.

How they the narrow Schoolroom dread and hate!

Sutler's Serving-Girl (entering).

They want to go, Aunt!

Cantinière.

Yes! directly dear!

First Chasseur.

Ay! Who's that little lass with saucy leer?

Cantinière.

My sister's child from Southern Germany. —

First Chasseur.

Ah! she's a lovely niece, by Geminy!

Second Chasseur (laying hold of the girl).

Now stay awhile with us, my charming Kate!

Sutler's Serving-Girl.

No! guests are there; so I must go and wait.

(disengages herself, and goes away.)

Erster Jäger.

Das Mädchen ist kein übler Bissen!
Und die Muhme — beim Element!
Was haben die Herrn vom Regiment
Sich um das niedliche Lärvchen gerissen!
Was man nicht alles für Leute kennt,
Und wie die Zeit von dannen rennt. —
Was werd' ich noch alles erleben müssen!

(Zum Wachtmeister und Trompeter.)

Euch zur Gesundheit, meine Herrn! —
Laßt uns hier auch ein Plätzchen nehmen.

Sechster Auftritt.

Jäger. Wachtmeister. Trompeter.

Wachtmeister.

Wir danken schön. Von Herzen gern.
Wir rücken zu. Willkommen in Böhmen!

Erster Jäger.

Ihr sitzt hier warm. Wir, in Feindes Land,
Mußten derweil uns schlecht bequemen.

Trompeter.

Man sollt's euch nicht ansehn, ihr seid galant.

Wachtmeister.

Ja, ja, im Saalskreis und auch in Meißen
Hört man euch Herrn nicht besonders preisen.

Zweiter Jäger.

Seid mir doch still! Was will das heißen?
Der Kroat es ganz anders trieb,
Uns nur die Nachles' übrig blieb.

First Chasseur.

That girl's a nice tit-bit — a darling love!
Her Aunt was too — by all the pow'rs above!
How once our Reg'ment — Officers and all —
About that pretty face did flounce and brawl!
Men of all sorts and kinds we come across!
And Time flies quickly by without remorse.
Ah! What events must I yet live to see!

(To the Serjeant-Major and the Trumpeter.

Good health. Sirs! please make room for him and me.

Scene VI.

Chasseurs. — Serjeant-Major. Trumpeter.

Serjeant-Major.

Thank ye! With all my heart! Close in all hands!
Comrades! you're welcome in Bohemia's lands!

First Chasseur.

Here snug and warm you keep — whilst we 'mongst foes
In hostile lands can hardly find repose.

Trumpeter.

One can't perceive it — you're so spruce and gay.

Serjeant-Major.

In Meissen and around the Saal. they say.
You were n't much priz'd. where'er you hung your hat.

Second Chasseur.

Still! hold your peace! — Pray what d'ye mean by that?
The Croat work'd quite otherwise. I'll swear.
They left us naught but gleanings for our share.

Trompeter.

Ihr habt da einen saubern Spitzen
Am Kragen, und wie euch die Hosen sitzen!
Die feine Wäsche, der Federhut!
Was das alles für Wirkung thut!
Daß doch den Burschen das Glück soll scheinen,
Und so was kommt nie an unser Einen!

Wachtmeister.

Dafür sind wir des Friedländers Regiment,
Man muß uns ehren und respectiren.

Erster Jäger.

Das ist für uns andre kein Compliment,
Wir eben so gut seinen Namen führen.

Wachtmeister.

Ja, ihr gehört auch so zur ganzen Masse.

Erster Jäger.

Ihr seid wohl von einer besondern Rasse?
Der ganze Unterschied ist in den Röcken,
Und ich ganz gern mag in meinem stecken.

Wachtmeister.

Herr Jäger, ich muß euch nur bedauern,
Ihr lebt so draußen bei den Bauern;
Der feine Griff und der rechte Ton,
Das lernt sich nur um des Feldherrn Person.

Erster Jäger.

Sie bekam euch übel, die Lection.
Wie er räuspert, und wie er spuckt,
Das habt ihr ihm glücklich abgeguckt;
Aber sein Schenie, ich meine, sein Geist
Sich nicht auf der Wachparade weist.

Trumpeter.

You sport there on your collar lace well knit.
And points; but how superb your breeches fit!
Your linen fine and feather'd hat are flash!
But don't they serve at least to cut a dash?

(To Serjeant-Major.)

That on those lads good luck may shine, this fuss
Is made; but such ne'er comes to one of us!

Serjeant-Major.

For we are Friedland's Reg'ment! And expect
That all will show us honour and respect.

First Chasseur.

To us all that's no compliment you pay;
We bear his name the same in ev'ry way.

Serjeant-Major.

Yes — with the common herd you take your place.

First Chasseur.

You're bred and born then of a diff'rent race?
The only diff'rence seems your coat so fine,
For my part I would sooner stick in mine.

Serjeant-Major.

Chasseur! I pity sooth your want of tact!
Living with boors such habits you contract;
Good manners and *bon-ton*, — 't is my belief,
Are only learnt when always 'bout our Chief.

First Chasseur.

The lessons, though improving they may be,
Did you no good, as far as I can see.
But how he hawks and how he spits about,
For imitation that you've soon pick'd out.
His genius rare — his vig'rous mind — I mean,
At mounting-guard-parade can ne'er be seen.

Zweiter Jäger.

Wetter auch! wo ihr nach uns fragt,
Wir heißen des Friedländers wilde Jagd
Und machen dem Namen keine Schande —
Ziehen frech durch Feindes und Freundes Lande,
Querfeldein durch die Saat, durch das gelbe Korn —
Sie kennen das Holk'sche Jägerhorn! —
In einem Augenblick fern und nah,
Schnell wie die Sündfluth, so sind wir da —
Wie die Feuerflamme bei dunkler Nacht
In die Häuser fähret, wenn niemand wacht —
Da hilft keine Gegenwehr, keine Flucht,
Keine Ordnung gilt mehr und keine Zucht. —
Es sträubt sich — der Krieg hat kein Erbarmen —
Das Mägdlein in unsern sehnigten Armen —
Fragt nach, ich sag's nicht, um zu prahlen;
In Baireuth, im Voigtland, in Westphalen,
Wo wir nur durchgekommen sind —
Erzählen Kinder und Kindeskind
Nach hundert und aber hundert Jahren
Von dem Holk noch und seinen Schaaren.

Wachtmeister.

Nun, da sieht man's! Der Saus und Braus,
Macht denn der den Soldaten aus?
Das Tempo macht ihn, der Sinn und Schick,
Der Begriff, die Bedeutung, der feine Blick.

Erster Jäger.

Die Freiheit macht ihn. Mit euren Fratzen!
Daß ich mit euch soll darüber schwatzen —
Lief ich darum aus der Schul' und der Lehre,
Daß ich die Frohn' und die Galeere,

Second Chasseur.

Where'er, my lads! you ask about us — 'Zounds!
We're known as Friedland's own wild pack of hounds;
And on that name we never bring disgrace —
Or foe's or friend's — we dash through ev'ry place.
Across sown-fields or through the yellow corn —
All know the sounds of Holk's shrill bugle-horn!
Then in a moment both from far and near,
Quick as the deluge, there we all appear —
As in night's darkness flames of fire soon fly
From house to house, when hush'd's the watchman's cry —
No help affords resistance; flight will fail;
Order and discipline will naught avail. —
The virgin struggles — War no pity feels —
And in our sinewy arms in vain appeals —
Ask after us — I say it not to boast —
In Bayreuth, or in Voigtland, or in most
Parts of Westphalia. — sooth where'er we came —
There children's children e'er will know our name,
Our deeds relate in centuries untold
And speak of Holk and of his hunters bold!

Serjeant - Major.

Fluster and bluster then! For they, I find,
Are qualities to frame the soldier's mind!
No! they're address, exactness, common-sense,
Foresight, *coup d'œil*, and great intelligence.

First Chasseur.

True freedom forms him best! — What twattling rot!
Why prate with you about it like a sot? —
Did I from books and school then bolt away
To drudge at taskwork, as a slave, all day,

Die Schreibstub' und ihre engen Wände
In dem Feldlager wiederfände? —
Flott will ich leben und müßig gehn,
Alle Tage was Neues sehn,
Mich dem Augenblick frisch vertrauen,
Nicht zurück, auch nicht vorwärts schauen —
Drum hab' ich meine Haut dem Kaiser verhandelt,
Daß keine Sorg' mich mehr anwandelt.
Führt mich ins Feuer frisch hinein,
Ueber den reißenden, tiefen Rhein —
Der dritte Mann soll verloren sein;
Werde mich nicht lang sperren und zieren. —
Sonst muß man mich aber, ich bitte sehr,
Mit nichts weiter incommodiren.

Wachtmeister.

Nu, nu, verlangt ihr sonst nichts mehr?
Das ließ sich unter dem Wamms da finden.

Erster Jäger.

Was war das nicht für ein Placken und Schinden
Bei Gustav, dem Schweden, dem Leuteplager!
Der machte eine Kirch' aus seinem Lager,
Ließ Betstunde halten, des Morgens, gleich
Bei der Reveille und beim Zapfenstreich.
Und wurden wir manchmal ein wenig munter,
Er kanzelt' uns selbst wohl vom Gaul herunter.

Wachtmeister.

Ja, es war ein gottesfürchtiger Herr.

Erster Jäger.

Dirnen, die ließ er gar nicht passiren,
Mußten sie gleich zur Kirche führen.
Da lief ich, konnt's nicht ertragen mehr.

The pen in narrow schoolroom 'gain to wield,
When once in quarters or encamp'd in field?
An idle jolly life I want to lead,
On something new each day my eye to feed;
For pleasures on the Present to hold fast,
Not looking to the Future or the Past —
Wherefore to Kaiser I have sold my hide,
That no more cares henceforth may be betide.
Lead me quick into fire — where'er it gleam —
Quick o'er old father Rhine's deep-gushing stream,
Ev'ry third man, I vow, shall surely fall!
I'll not be shy and long resist the call. —
Beyond such matters then — I must implore —
That you'll not incommode me any more.
                Serjeant-Major.
Well then! If that is all you want, you will
Perhaps beneath your doublet find it still!
                First Chasseur.
What turmoils and exactions we had then
Under the Swede, Gustavus, plague of Men!
Into a Church he quick transform'd his camp,
And shed on all new light from Luther's lamp;
To pray'r Reveille's call forc'd all to come,
Again we pray'd at Tattoo's beat of drum.
Were we at times much gayer than we need,
He preach'd to us himself from off his steed.
                Serjeant-Major.
He was a pious and God-fearing King.
                First Chasseur.
Wenches in camp no soldier dar'd to bring,
Unless to altar quick he led the slut.
I could no longer stand it; so I cut.

Wachtmeister.

Jetzt geht's dort auch wohl anders her.

Erster Jäger.

So ritt ich hinüber zu den Liguisten,
Sie thäten sich just gegen Magdeburg rüsten.
Ja, das war schon ein ander Ding!
Alles da lustiger, loser ging,
Soff und Spiel und Mädels die Menge!
Wahrhaftig, der Spaß war nicht gering,
Denn der Tilly verstand sich aufs Kommandieren.
Dem eigenen Körper war er strenge,
Dem Soldaten ließ er Vieles passieren,
Und ging's nur nicht aus seiner Kassen,
Sein Spruch war: leben und leben lassen.
Aber das Glück war ihm nicht stät —
Seit der Leipziger Fatalität
Wollt' es eben nirgends mehr flecken,
Alles bei uns gerieth ins Stecken;
Wo wir erschienen und pochten an,
Ward nicht gegrüßt noch aufgethan.
Wir mußten uns drücken von Ort zu Ort,
Der alte Respect war eben fort. —
Da nahm ich Handgeld von den Sachsen,
Meinte, da müßte mein Glück recht wachsen.

Wachtmeister.

Nun, da kamt ihr ja eben recht
Zur böhmischen Beute.

Erster Jäger.

Es ging mir schlecht.
Sollten da strenge Mannszucht halten,
Durften nicht recht als Feinde walten,

Serjeant-Major.

How chang'd is all! Now reigns a diff'rent mode!

First Chasseur.

So to the Leaguer's Camp away I rode,
As they 'gainst Magdeburg were arming still.
'T was quite another thing! We took our fill
Of joy! Much gayer — merrier lives we spent
With drink, play, wenches to our heart's content!
Pastimes forsooth were countless as the sand.
For Tilly knew right well how to command;
From stringent rules himself he never shields
Whilst to the soldiers he much licence yields,
And spends fast save from his own treasure-chest —
"Live and let live!" — he lik'd that proverb best. —
To him good fortune prov'd a fickle mate; —
For since at Leipsic that disastrous fate,
No where could we get on in any land,
All things collaps'd and brought us to a stand;
Where'er we near'd in sight — where'er we knock'd —
No greeting came — nor was a gate unlock'd;
We had to slip away from place to place,
The old respect was lost and left no trace. —
So from the Saxons I press-money took
Thinking to seize good-luck by hook and crook.

Serjeant-Major.

Just in the nick of time you came for our
Bohemian booty.

First Chasseur.

　　　　Times were hard and sour.
Here forc'd the strictest discipline to keep
O'er ev'ry place, as foes, we dar'd not sweep;

Mußten des Kaisers Schlösser bewachen.
Viel Umständ' und Complimente machen,
Führten den Krieg, als wär's nur Scherz,
Hatten für die Sach nur ein halbes Herz,
Wollten's mit niemand ganz verderben,
Kurz, da war wenig Ehr zu erwerben,
Und ich wär' bald für Ungeduld
Wieder heimgelaufen zum Schreibepult,
Wenn nicht eben auf allen Straßen
Der Friedländer hätte werben lassen.

Wachtmeister.

Und wie lang denkt ihr's hier auszuhalten?

Erster Jäger.

Spaßt nur! So lange der thut walten,
Denk' ich euch, mein Seel! an kein Entlaufen.
Kann's der Soldat wo besser kaufen? —
Da geht alles nach Kriegessitt',
Hat alles 'nen großen Schnitt,
Und der Geist, der im ganzen Corps thut leben,
Reißet gewaltig, wie Windesweben,
Auch den untersten Reiter mit.
Da tret' ich auf mit beherztem Schritt,
Darf über den Bürger kühn wegschreiten,
Wie der Feldherr über der Fürsten Haupt.
Es ist hier wie in den alten Zeiten,
Wo die Klinge noch alles thät bedeuten;
Da gibt's nur ein Vergehn und Verbrechen:
Der Ordre fürwitzig widersprechen.
Was nicht verboten ist, ist erlaubt;
Da fragt niemand, was einer glaubt.
Es gibt nur zwei Ding' überhaupt:

But must the Kaiser's castles watch around,
Where lots of pageants and salutes abound,
In war, as if in jest, we play'd our part,
For such things we had only half a heart,
We wish'd with none a lasting breach to leave,
In short! there little fame could we achieve;
Impatient with this state of things I fain
Would have return'd to writing-desk again,
Had I not then been doom'd in ev'ry street
Friedland's recruiting Serjeants e'er to meet.

Serjeant-Major.

How long with us do you expect to stay?

First Chasseur.

You jest! As long as he holds firm his sway,
I ne'er could dream his banner to forsake.
Where could a better contract soldiers make?
For here to War's strict customs all adhere,
All things 'a grand and noble impress bear,
And the *esprit*, that lives throughout the Corps,
Stirs all with whirlwind's fury more and more,
Till piercing e'en the humblest Rider's breast.
Then I with proudly gait step out my best
And rough-shod o'er civilians dare to ride,
As loves our Chief o'er Princes' heads to stride.
'T is here at present as in times of old,
When the bare sword alone its will fortold:
One crime — one misdemeanor 's only known,
To speak 'gainst Orders in a saucy tone!
That, which is not forbidden, is allow'd;
None asks to what religion you have vow'd.
In fact two kind of things we 've only got,

Was zur Armee gehört und nicht;
Und nur der Fahne bin ich verpflicht.

Wachtmeister.

Jetzt gefallt ihr mir, Jäger! Ihr sprecht
Wie ein Friedländischer Reitersknecht.

Erster Jäger.

Der führt's Kommando nicht wie ein Amt,
Wie eine Gewalt, die vom Kaiser stammt!
Es ist ihm nicht um des Kaisers Dienst,
Was bracht' er dem Kaiser für Gewinnst?
Was hat er mit seiner großen Macht
Zu des Landes Schirm und Schutz vollbracht?
Ein Reich von Soldaten wollt' er gründen,
Die Welt anstecken und entzünden,
Sich alles vermessen und unterwinden —

Trompeter.

Still, wer wird solche Worte wagen!

Erster Jäger.

Was ich denke, das darf ich sagen.
Das Wort ist frei, sagt der General. ·

Wachtmeister.

So sagt er, ich hört's wohl einigemal,
Ich stand dabei. „Das Wort ist frei,
„Die That ist stumm, der Gehorsam blind,"
Dies urkundlich seine Worte sind.

Erster Jäger.

Ob's just seine Wort' sind, weiß ich nicht;
Aber die Sach' ist so, wie er spricht.

Zweiter Jäger.

Ihm schlägt das Kriegsglück nimmer um,
Wie's wohl bei andern pflegt zu geschehen

And one the Army claims — the other not.
Allegiance to our flag I only owe.

Serjeant-Major.

Chasseur! You please me now! You speak just so,
As one of Friedland's horsemen ought to speak.

First Chasseur.

For he commands not like a steward meek
And servile, who to Kaiser owes his pow'r!
For Kaiser self he would not serve an hour.
What mighty gains has he to Kaiser brought?
His pow'r — what safety to our lands has wrought?
But he a state of soldiers long'd to found;
Then set the world on fire; burn all around;
Measure with all; dare all; and all subdue —
All that blends not with his ambitious view —

Trumpeter.

Who dares such words to utter, whilst I live?

First Chasseur.

Of what I think, bold utt'rance I will give.
For speech is free — so said our noble Chief.

Serjeant-Major.

I heard him often, 't is my firm belief,
As I stood by, thus saying — "Speech is free,
Deed is dumb, and obedience blind must be."
These are his very words, I know them well.

First Chasseur.

Whether these words are his, I cannot tell;
But plain 's the fact, that he so well express'd.

Second Chasseur.

In war ill-fortune ne'er his soul oppress'd,
Like others, who to grief so often came.

3 *

Der Tilly überlebte seinen Ruhm.
Doch unter des Friedländers Kriegspanieren,
Da bin ich gewiß zu victorisiren.
Er bannet das Glück, es muß ihm stehen.
Wer unter seinem Zeichen thut fechten,
Der steht unter besondern Mächten.
Denn das weiß ja die ganze Welt,
Daß der Friedländer einen Teufel
Aus der Hölle im Solde hält.

Wachtmeister.

Ja, daß er fest ist, das ist kein Zweifel;
Denn in der blut'gen Affaire bei Lützen
Ritt er euch unter des Feuers Blitzen
Auf und nieder mit kühlem Blut.
Durchlöchert von Kugeln war sein Hut,
Durch den Stiefel und Koller fuhren
Die Ballen, man sah die deutlichen Spuren;
Konnt' ihm keine die Haut nur ritzen,
Weil ihn die höllische Salbe thät schützen.

Erster Jäger.

Was wollt ihr da für Wunder bringen!
Er trägt ein Koller von Elendshaut,
Das keine Kugel kann durchdringen.

Wachtmeister.

Nein, es ist die Salbe von Hexenkraut,
Unter Zaubersprüchen gekocht und gebraut.

Trompeter.

Es geht nicht zu mit rechten Dingen!

Wachtmeister.

Sie sagen, er les' auch in den Sternen
Die künftigen Dinge, die nahen und fernen;

In truth brave Tilly did o'erlive his fame.
But under Friedland's banners, I maintain,
That vict'ry 's sure to follow in our train.
Good luck he conjurs up and holds in sight;
For he, who wears his badge, and fain would fight,
Stands under special influence and pow'r;
The world knows well his strange and mystic low'r,
And that our Friedland has a Dev'l in hell,
Whom he retains in pay to use his spell.

Serjeant - Major.

He is invulnerable, there's no doubt.
On Lützen's bloody field naught put him out;
Calm and unmov'd he rode through thickest fire
Amidst the ranks — their courage to inspire.
Forsooth his hat with balls was pierc'd right through,
One saw the marks on boots and jerkih, too;
But on his skin no scratch could they effect,
Because a hellish salve did him protect.

First Chasseur.

What wonders, you profess, in him abide!
He wears a jerkin made of moose - deer's hide,
Through which a bullet ne'er can penetrate.

Serjeant - Major.

No — 't is a salve of herbs, that witches late
At night with incantations have prepared.

Trumpeter.

To join in things unhallow'd he has dar'd!

Serjeant - Major.

'T is said, that he can read in ev'ry star
All future things, should they be near or far;

Ich weiß aber besser, wie's damit ist.
Ein graues Männlein pflegt bei nächtlicher Frist
Durch verschlossene Thüren zu ihm einzugehen;
Die Schildwachen haben's oft angeschrien,
Und immer was Großes ist drauf geschehen,
Wenn je das graue Röcklein kam und erschien.

Zweiter Jäger.

Ja, er hat sich dem Teufel übergeben,
Drum führen wir auch das lustige Leben.

Siebenter Auftritt.

Vorige. Ein Rekrut. Ein Bürger. Dragoner.

Rekrut

(tritt aus dem Zelte, eine Blechhaube auf dem Kopfe, eine Weinflasche in der Hand.)

Grüß den Vater' und Vaters Brüder!
Bin Soldat, komme nimmer wieder.

Erster Jäger.

Sieh, da bringen sie einen Neuen!

Bürger.

O, gib Acht, Franz, es wird dich reuen.

Rekrut (singt).

Trommeln und Pfeifen,
Kriegerischer Klang!
Wandern und streifen
Die Welt entlang,
Rosse gelenkt,
Muthig geschwenkt,
Schwert an der Seite,
Frisch in die Weite,
Flüchtig und flink,

But I know better what is true and right.
A greyish dwarf is wont at dead of night
Entrance to him through bolted doors to gain;
Oft watchful sentries challeng'd him in vain;
And always something great has happen'd then,
When this Grey-Coat appear'd within his ken.

Second Chasseur.

Ay! To old Nick he's sold himself indeed
And therefore such a jolly life we lead.

Scene VII.

The above. — Recruit. — Citizen. — Dragoons.

Recruit

(advancing from the tent with a metal-headpiece on his head and
a wine-flask in his hand.)

My father and my father's brothers greet!
I'm soldier now — them ne'er again I'll meet.

First Chasseur.

See! a new-hand they bring — there's lots of cash!

Citizen.

Oh! Frank! take care — you'll rue this act so rash.

Recruit (sings).

With drum and fife,
   That warlike sound!
We march for strife
   The world around!
Steeds well in hand,
Wheel'd at command,
Sword by the side,
O'er far and wide
We ride the pace,

Frei, wie der Fink
Auf Sträuchern und Bäumen
In Himmels-Räumen,
Heisa! ich folge des Friedländers Fahn'!

Zweiter Jäger.

Seht mir, das ist ein wackrer Rumpan!
(Sie begrüßen ihn.)

Bürger.

O, laßt ihn! er ist guter Leute Kind.

Erster Jäger.

Wir auch nicht auf der Straße gefunden sind.

Bürger.

Ich sag' euch, er hat Vermögen und Mittel.
Fühlt her, das feine Tüchlein am Kittel!

Trompeter.

Des Kaisers Rock ist der höchste Titel.

Bürger.

Er erbt eine kleine Mützenfabrik.

Zweiter Jäger.

Des Menschen Wille, das ist sein Glück.

Bürger.

Von der Großmutter einen Kram und Laden.

Erster Jäger.

Pfui, wer handelt mit Schwefelfaden!

Bürger.

Einen Weinschank dazu von seiner Pathen,
Ein Gewölbe mit zwanzig Stückfaß Wein.

Trompeter.

Den theilt er mit seinen Kameraden.

Zweiter Jäger.

Hör' du! wir müssen Zeltbrüder sein.

As chaffinch free
From bush to tree
Darts through the airy space
Hurrah! I follow Friedland's banner!

Second Chasseur.

Look! He's a jolly comrade, I'll be sworn!

(They greet him.)

Citizen.

Pray! leave him — he's of honest parents born.

First Chasseur.

But we ourselves were n't pick'd from off the street.

Citizen.

He is well off indeed — I must repeat; —
Just feel the texture of the cloth he wears.

Trumpeter.

The Kaiser's coat the highest title bears.

Citizen.

To a Cap-Maker's business he is heir.

Second Chasseur.

On man's own will depends his fortune e'er.

Citizen.

From his Grandam descends a retail-shop —

First Chasseur.

Fy! Who would deal in matches and in pop!

Citizen.

His Godmother bequeaths a tavern fine,
And cellar fill'd with twenty butts of wine.

Trumpeter.

Ah! These he with his comrades will divide.

Second Chasseur.

Come, share my tent — we'll live there side by side!

Bürger.

Eine Braut läßt er sitzen in Thränen und Schmerz.

Erster Jäger.

Recht so, da zeigt er ein eisernes Herz.

Bürger.

Die Großmutter wird für Kummer sterben.

Zweiter Jäger.

Desto besser, so kann er sie gleich beerben.

Wachtmeister.

(tritt gravitätisch hinzu, dem Rekruten die Hand auf die Blechhaube legend.)

Sieht Er! Das hat Er wohl erwogen.

Einen neuen Menschen hat Er angezogen;

Mit dem Helm da und Wehrgehäng

Schließt Er sich an eine würdige Meng'.

Muß ein fürnehmer Geist jetzt in Ihn fahren —

Erster Jäger.

Muß besonders das Geld nicht sparen.

Wachtmeister.

Auf der Fortuna ihrem Schiff

Ist Er zu segeln im Begriff;

Die Weltkugel liegt vor Ihm offen.

Wer nichts waget, der darf nichts hoffen.

Es treibt sich der Bürgersmann, träg und dumm,

Wie des Färbers Gaul, nur im Ring herum.

Aus dem Soldaten kann alles werden,

Denn Krieg ist jetzt die Losung auf Erden.

Seh' Er 'mal mich an! In diesem Rock

Führ' ich, sieht Er, des Kaisers Stock.

Citizen.

A bride in grief and tears he leaves behind.

First Chasseur.

That shows an iron heart — unbending mind.

Citizen.

Grandma will die of grief at such a fall.

Second Chasseur.

Much better — he can then inherit all.

Serjeant-Major.

(advancing gravely places his hand upon the Recruit's metal head-piece.)

Young fellow, look! You've weigh'd the matter well.

New life will gush forth from your mortal shell.

With helmet on and sword upon your hip

Now in amongst a worthy crew you'll slip;

A noble spirit must light up now your soul —

First Chasseur.

Must spend your tin, and blithesome pass the bowl.

Serjeant - Major.

On Fortune's ship — capricious Goddess e'er!

Embark'd, you'll hoist your sail with votive pray'r.

Now the wide-world lies open to your view;

Who ventures naught, dares naught with hope pursue.

Dull works the cit — in narrow limits bound —

Just as the dyer's jade goes round and round.

The soldier's glory can no limit know,

For War's the only watchword here below.

Look ye! — Here at my jacket look again!

I wear the Kaiser's badge — the Serjeant's cane.*)

---

*) The grade of Serjeant-Major and Serjeant was distinguished in the Imperial Austrian Service by a *cane* attached to the Jacket by a leathern sling; that of a Corporal by a *stick* of inferior wood. Chevrons or other distinctive marks were formerly not used.

Alles Weltregiment, muß Er wissen,
Von dem Stock hat ausgehen müssen;
Und das Scepter in Königs Hand
Ist ein Stock nur, das ist bekannt.
Und wer's zum Korporal erst hat gebracht,
Der steht auf der Leiter zur höchsten Macht,
Und so weit kann Er's auch noch treiben.

Erster Jäger.
Wenn Er nur lesen kann und schreiben.

Wachtmeister.
Da will ich Ihm gleich ein Exempel geben;
Ich thät's vor Kurzem selbst erleben.
Da ist der Schef vom Dragonercorps,
Heißt Buttler, wir standen als Gemeine
Noch vor dreißig Jahren bei Köln am Rheine,
Jetzt nennt man ihn Generalmajor.
Das macht, er thät sich baß hervor,
Thät die Welt mit seinem Kriegsruhm füllen;
Doch meine Verdienste, die blieben im Stillen.
Ja, und der Friedländer selbst, sieht Er,
Unser Hauptmann und hochgebietender Herr,
Der jetzt alles vermag und kann,
War erst nur ein schlichter Edelmann,
Und weil er der Kriegsgöttin sich vertraut,
Hat er sich diese Größ' erbaut,
Ist nach dem Kaiser der nächste Mann,
Und wer weiß, was er noch erreicht und ermißt,
(Pfiffig.) Denn noch nicht aller Tage Abend ist.

Erster Jäger.
Ja, er fing's klein an und ist jetzt so groß!

All worldly rule and pow'r — I need not state —
Must always from the cane originate;
'T is known — the sceptre in the King's right-hand
Is but a cane, that governs all the land!
He, who on Corp'rals' roll once bears his name,
Stands on the ladder to the highest fame;
And also you may mount this topmost height.

First Chasseur.
Forsooth! If he can only read and write.

Serjeant-Major.
Th' example now I'll set before your eyes,
Which I've just liv'd to see — time swiftly flies.
There's Butler — he of our Dragoons the Chief
Who oft, as Private, rode in my relief,
Gone thirty years, beneath Cologne's high wall.
As Major-Gen'ral now salute him all!
That comes from having carv'd himself a name,
And fill'd the world with wonder at his fame:
My services — however great and long —
In stillness sleep and wake not glory's song.
Yes! Friedland self — so Hist'ry doth record, —
Who's now our Captain and all-ruling Lord,
And all disposes as he will and can,
Was t'other day a simple Gentleman.
Since he to War's stern Goddess pledg'd his faith,
His greatness he has built, where all was scath;
After the Kaiser he's the next great man;
And who then knows what he may reach or scan?
(Cunningly.) For evening brings to close not ev'ry day!

First Chasseur.
Though small at first — now potent is his sway.

Denn zu Altorf im Studentenkragen,
Trieb er's, mit Permiß zu sagen,
Ein wenig locker und burschikos,
Hätte seinen Famulus bald erschlagen.
Wollten ihn drauf die Nürnberger Herren
Mir nichts, dir nichts ins Carcer sperren;
's war just ein neugebautes Nest,
Der erste Bewohner sollt' es taufen.
Aber wie fängt er's an? Er läßt
Weislich den Pudel voran erst laufen.
Nach dem Hunde nennt sich's bis diesen Tag;
Ein rechter Kerl sich dran spiegeln mag.
Unter des Herrn großen Thaten allen
Hat mir das Stückchen besonders gefallen.

(Das Mädchen hat unterdessen aufgewartet; der zweite Jäger schäkert
mit ihr.)

Dragoner (tritt dazwischen).
Kamerad, laß Er das unterwegen!

Zweiter Jäger.
Wer Henker! hat sich da drein zu legen?

Dragoner.
Ich will's Ihm nur sagen, die Dirn' ist mein.

Erster Jäger.
Der will ein Schätzchen für sich allein!
Dragoner, ist Er bei Troste? sag' Er!

Zweiter Jäger.
Will was Apartes haben im Lager.
Einer Dirne schön Gesicht
Muß allgemein sein, wie's Sonnenlicht!
(Küßt sie.)

Dragoner (reißt sie weg).
Ich sag's noch einmal, das leid' ich nicht.

At Altdorf, when in Student's cap and gown,
He went the pace too fast for that staid town;
In larks and sprees no seemly bounds he knew,
And once his Servitor he nearly slew.
At Nürenberg the Bigwigs umbrage took
And wish'd to cage him too by hook and crook.
The prison must — a new-built airy nest —
Be nam'd by the first lodger-in-arrest.
But how sets he to work? His poodle, Rose,
He wisely lets run in before his nose.
After his dog the prison's call'd this day.
Smart chaps might take a wrinkle from such play.
But all our Hero's great and wondrous feats
This cunning dodge, me seems, all hollow beats!

(The Sutler's girl has in the meanwhile served up; and the Second
Chasseur begins to jest and toy with her.)

Dragoon (stepping between them).

Now, Comrade! leave her; let that matter be!

Second Chasseur.

Pray! who the deuce dares interfere with me?

Dragoon.

I plainly tell you, that the girl is mine.

First Chasseur.

You 'll keep this treasure to yourself -- that's fine!
Tell me, Dragoon! Are you in your right mind?

Second Chasseur.

A thing apart in Camp you fain would find.
A girl's sweet face must common be to all,
As sunbeams e'er on all alike will fall.

(Kisses her.)

Dragoon (tears her away).

Once more I tell you, that I will not bear.

Erster Jäger.

Lustig, lustig! da kommen die Prager!

Zweiter Jäger.

Sucht er Händel? Ich bin dabei.

Wachtmeister.

Fried', ihr Herren! Ein Kuß ist frei!

Achter Auftritt.

Bergknappen treten auf und spielen einen Walzer, erst langsam und dann immer geschwinder. Der erste Jäger tanzt mit der Aufwärterin, die Marketenderin mit dem Rekruten; das Mädchen entspringt, der Jäger hinter ihr her und bekommt den Kapuziner zu fassen, der eben hereintritt.

Kapuziner.

Heisa, Juchheisa! Dudeldumdei!
Das geht ja hoch her. Bin auch dabei!
Ist das eine Armee von Christen?
Sind wir Türken? sind wir Antibaptisten?
Treibt man so mit dem Sonntag Spott,
Als hätte der allmächtige Gott
Das Chiragra, könnte nicht drein schlagen?
Ist's jetzt Zeit zu Saufgelagen,
Zu Banketten und Feiertagen?
Quid hic statis otiosi?
Was steht ihr und legt die Hände in Schooß?
Die Kriegsfurie ist an der Donau los,
Das Bollwerk des Bayerlands ist gefallen,
Regensburg ist in des Feindes Krallen,
Und die Armee liegt hier in Böhmen,
Pflegt den Bauch, läßt sich's wenig grämen,

First Chasseur.

Come on, my boys! there come the Pragners here!

Second Chasseur.

Seek ye a quarrel? I your man will be.

Serjeant-Major.

Peace — Sirs! To all a kiss is ever free!

Scene VIII.

Enter Miners and play a Waltz — at first slowly and then faster and faster. The First Chasseur dances with the Sutler's serving-girl, the Cantinière with the Recruit. — The girl springs away, the Chasseur pursues her and seizes hold of a Capuchin Friar just entering.

Capuchin Friar.

Huzzah! Hurrah! Ri tooral looral loo!
'T is pretty jolly here! I'll join in too!
Is this an army of true Christians here?
As Turks or Anabaptists we appear!
That we so scoff our Sunday's day of rest.
As if our God Almighty were oppress'd
With gout, and could not join this festive rout!
Is this the time for such a drinking bout,
For banquets, and our Church's holy-day?
"*Quid hic statis otiosi?*" I say —
Why stand you idle here with folded arms?
The Furies sound on Danube war's alarms,
Bavaria's bulwark is just fallen low,
Ratisbon's in the clutches of our foe;
And here the Army in Bohemia rests,.
Feeds well, nor frets for higher interests;

4

Kümmert sich mehr um den Krug als den Krieg,
Wetzt lieber den Schnabel als den Säbel,
Hetzt sich lieber herum mit der Dirn',
Frißt den Ochsen lieber als den Oxenstirn.
Die Christenheit trauert in Sack und Asche,
Der Soldat füllt sich nur die Tasche.
Es ist eine Zeit der Thränen und Noth,
Am Himmel geschehen Zeichen und Wunder,
Und aus den Wolken, blutigroth,
Hängt der Herrgott den Kriegsmantel 'runter.
Den Kometen steckt er, wie eine Ruthe,
Drohend am Himmelsfenster aus,
Die ganze Welt ist ein Klagehaus,
Die Arche der Kirche schwimmt in Blute,
Und das römische Reich — daß Gott erbarm!
Sollte jetzt heißen römisch Arm;
Der Rheinstrom ist worden zu einem Peinstrom.
Die Klöster sind ausgenommene Nester,
Die Bisthümer sind verwandelt in Wüstthümer,
Die Abteien und die Stifter
Sind nun Raubteien und Diebesklüfter,
Und alle die gesegneten deutschen Länder
Sind verkehrt worden in Elender —
Woher kommt das? Das will ich euch verkünden:
Das schreibt sich her von euren Lastern und Sünden,
Von dem Gräuel und Heidenleben,
Dem sich Officier und Soldaten ergeben.
Denn die Sünd' ist der Magnetenstein,
Der das Eisen ziehet ins Land herein.
Auf das Unrecht, da folgt das Uebel,

The *jug* more *joy* than war will all afford;
They *whet* the *whistle* rather than the *sword;*
They hunt the *vixens* rather than the *fox,*
Instead of *Oxenstiern* they roast the *ox.*
Christians in sackcloth and in ashes weep,
While soldiers fill their pockets at one sweep.
This is a time of tears, distress and fear,
For signs and wonders in the skies appear,
And now from clouds — blood-red — the Lord of all
War's mantle spreads below o'er great and small.
A comet stands in heaven's casement wide
Portentous like a rod to scourge our pride;
A house of mourning is this wicked world;
Through streams of blood our Church's ark is whirl'd;
The *Roman Empire* — God protect the same! —
To stand as *Roman Umpire* must disclaim;
The *Rhine* will *pine* and ebb away with grief;
To *cloister* come to *roister* rogue and thief;
Bishop and *diocess* will *die or cease,*
Abbeys and *Minsters* welcome now in peace
Rabbis and *Ministers* of ev'ry faith;
And in the *blessed German States* now scath
And ruin o'erwhelm the *cursed German pates!* —
And wherefore thus? I'll tell you whence it dates —
From your great vices, sins, and constant strife,
Abominations, too, and heathen life;
For such is now, I grieve to say, the course,
All grades of soldiers lead without remorse.
For sin's the magnet-stone, that sure attracts
Your polish'd steel within our mountain-tracts.
For from injustice spring all ev'ls and cares,

4*

Wie die Thrän' auf den herben Zwiebel,
Hinter dem U kommt gleich das Weh,
Das ist die Ordnung im A B C.
Ubi erit victoriae spes,
Si offenditur Deus? Wie soll man siegen,
Wenn man die Predigt schwänzt und die Meß,
Nichts thut, als in den Weinhäusern liegen?
Die Frau in dem Evangelium
Fand den verlornen Groschen wieder,
Der Saul seines Vaters Esel wieder,
Der Joseph seine saubern Brüder;
Aber wer bei den Soldaten sucht
Die Furcht Gottes und die gute Zucht
Und die Scham, der wird nicht viel finden,
Thät' er auch hundert Laternen anzünden.
Zu dem Prediger in der Wüsten,
Wie wir   lesen im Evangelisten,
Kamen auch die Soldaten gelaufen,
Thaten Buß' und ließen sich taufen,
Fragten ihn: Quid faciemus nos?
Wie machen wir's, daß wir kommen in Abrahams Schooß?
Et ait illis, und er sagt:
Neminem concutiatis,
Wenn ihr niemanden schindet und plackt.
Neque calumniam faciatis,
Niemand verlästert, auf niemand lügt.
Contenti estote, euch begnügt,
Stipendiis vestris, mit eurer Löhnung
Und verflucht jede böse Angewöhnung.

As from fresh onions gush unwilling tears;
O follows N, and *no* creates much *woe!*
For A. B. C. must in that order go.
For "*ubi erit victoriæ spes,*
Si offenditur Deus?" State now, please,
How can we conquer and fresh laurels gain,
If from High-Mass and Sermon we abstain
To seek such pleasures, as low tipplers' haunts
Afford, where vice in gaudy squalor flaunts?
In Gospel sought the woman not in vain,
But found the missing piece of coin again;
So Saul again beheld his father's ass,
Joseph his brothers — thus it came to pass;
But, who in midst of soldiers seeks to find
The fear of God, a truly pious mind,
And discipline, will scarce descry a mite,
Although a hundred lamps his search might light.
But to the Preacher in the wilderness
Came even soldiers forth with willingness
Sins to confess, repent and be baptiz'd;
So Gospels taught, when we were catechis'd.
"*Quid faciemus nos*"? They ask'd, what test
Go through to find in Abr'ham's bosom rest?
"*Et ait illis*" And he saith to them
These words "*concutiatis neminem*"
Sore vex and persecute no man; and this
"*Neque calumniam faciatis,*"
Slander no man, nor calumnies invent;
"*Contenti estote*" — and be content
"*Stipendiis vestris*" — with your day's pay;
Cursed is he, who walks in sinful way.

Es ist ein Gebot: Du sollt den Namen
Deines Herrgotts nicht eitel auskramen!
Und wo hört man mehr blasphemieren,
Als hier in den Friedländischen Kriegsquartieren?
Wenn man für jeden Donner und Blitz,
Den ihr losbrennt mit eurer Zungenspitz,
Die Glocken müßt' läuten im Land umher,
Es wär' bald kein Meßner zu finden mehr.
Und wenn euch für jedes böse Gebet,
Das aus eurem ungewaschnen Munde geht,
Ein Härlein ausging aus eurem Schopf,
Ueber Nacht wär' er geschoren glatt,
Und wär' er so dick wie ein Absalons Zopf.
Der Josua war doch auch ein Soldat,
König David erschlug den Goliath,
Und wo steht denn geschrieben zu lesen,
Daß sie solche Fluchmäuler sind gewesen?
Muß man den Mund doch, ich sollte meinen,
Nicht weiter aufmachen zu einem Helf Gott!
Als zu einem Kreuz Sackerlot!
Aber wessen das Gefäß ist gefüllt,
Davon es sprudelt und überquillt.

 Wieder ein Gebot ist: Du sollt nicht stehlen.
Ja, das befolgt ihr nach dem Wort,
Denn ihr tragt alles offen fort.
Vor euren Klauen und Geiersgriffen,
Vor euren Praktiken und bösen Kniffen
Ist das Geld nicht geborgen in der Truh,
Das Kalb nicht sicher in der Kuh,
Ihr nehmt das Ei und das Huhn dazu.
Was sagt der Prediger? Contenti estote,

"Thou shalt not" (this commandment is quite plain)
"Take the name of the Lord thy God in vain;"
And where can one so much blaspheming hear
As in your Friedland's camp and quarters here?
Should ev'ry curse and ev'ry oath indeed,
That from your double-edged tongue proceed,
By peal of bells be known throughout the land,
Bell-ringers scarce enough would be at hand;
Each imprecation and each word obscene,
That dart like arrows from your mouth unclean,
Should from your head each cause a hair to fall,
Then in one night you would be shorn of all,
Were e'en the crop as thick as Absolom's. —
Joshua at times a soldier, too, becomes;
King David did the huge Goliath slay,
And in what book then stands it writ, I pray!
That they such foul-mouth'd coarse blasphemers were?
In my opinion then our lips should ne'er
Ope wider than "God bless you!" and, if meant
In joke, to "Holy Cross!" and "Sacrament!"
What fills a vessel to the brim will rise
In bubbles and o'erflow — whate'er its size.
And this commandment, too, "Thou shalt not steal,"
Is follow'd to the word, your deeds reveal;
You carry off all things in spite of laws.
For from your clutches and your vulture's claws,
And from your thievish tricks and cunning hands
No gold, though hid in chests, in safety stands;
In the cow's womb the calf is not secure;
You seize the egg and then the hen procure.
"Contenti estote" — the Preacher said,

Begnügt euch mit eurem Commißbrote.
Aber wie soll man die Knechte loben,
Kömmt doch das Aergerniß von oben!
Wie die Glieder, so auch das Haupt!
Weiß doch niemand, an wen der glaubt!

Erster Jäger.

Herr Pfaff! uns Soldaten mag Er schimpfen,
Den Feldherrn soll Er uns nicht verunglimpfen.

Kapuziner.

Ne custodias gregem meam!
Das ist so ein Ahab und Jerobeam,
Der die Völker von der wahren Lehren
Zu falschen Götzen thut verkehren.

Trompeter und Rekrut.

Laß Er uns das nicht zweimal hören!

Kapuziner.

So ein Bramarbas und Eisenfresser,
Will einnehmen alle festen Schlösser.
Rühmte sich mit seinem gottlosen Mund,
Er müsse haben die Stadt Stralsund,
Und wär' sie mit Ketten an den Himmel geschlossen.

Trompeter.

Stopft ihm keiner sein Lästermaul?

Kapuziner.

So ein Teufelsbeschwörer und König Saul,
So ein Jehu und Holofern,
Verleugnet, wie Petrus, seinen Meister und Herrn,
Drum kann er den Hahn nicht hören krähn —

Beide Jäger.

Pfaffe! Jetzt ist's um dich geschehn!

Kapuziner.

So ein listiger Fuchs Herodes —

Always be ye content with ration-bread.
But why should we the serving-men commend,
When all the ills from their great Lord descend?
As human members all the head obey!
But to what faith he holds, can no one say?

First Chasseur.

Your Rev'rence may bespatter with abuse
Soldiers, but spare our Chief from such misuse.

Capuchin Friar.

Pray! "*Ne custodias gregem meum*"
He is like Ahab and Jerobeam
Who turn'd their people from true Prophet's ways
Idols to worship and false gods to praise.

Trumpeter and Recruit.

Let us not hear a second time such trash!

Capuchin Friar.

Marry! This braggard and big bully 's rash
To boast with his ungodly tongue, no doubt,
That he can storm alone each strong redoubt;
That he could Stralsund take by mere assault
E'en if 't were bound by chains to heav'n's high vault!

Trumpeter.

I say! Will no one stop his sland'rous bawl?

Capuchin Friar.

Such an exorcist, and such a King Saul.
Such a John, and such a Holofern,
Like Peter, must 'gainst Lord and Master turn;
Wherefore no crowing of the cock he hears —

Both Chasseurs.

Priest! 'T is all up with you! So still your fears!

Capuchin Friar.

A fox as cunning as Herod was, I vow!

Trompeter und beide Jäger
(auf ihn eindringend).

Schweig stille! Du bist des Todes!

Kroaten (legen sich drein).

Bleib da, Pfäfflein, fürchte dich nit,
Sag dein Sprüchel und theil's uns mit.

Kapuziner (schreit lauter).

So ein hochmüthiger Nebucadnezer,
So ein Sündenvater und muffiger Ketzer,
Läßt sich nennen den Wallenstein;
Ja freilich ist er uns allen ein Stein
Des Anstoßes und Aergernisses,
Und so lang der Kaiser diesen Friedeland
Läßt walten, so wird nicht Fried' im Land.

(Er hat nach und nach bei den letzten Worten, die er mit erhobener Stimme
spricht, seinen Rückzug genommen, indem die Kroaten die übrigen Soldaten
von ihm abwehren.)

Neunter Auftritt.

Vorige, ohne den Kapuziner.

Erster Jäger (zum Wachtmeister).

Sagt mir, was meint' er mit dem Göckelhahn,
Den der Feldherr nicht krähen hören kann?
Es war wohl nur so gesagt ihm zum Schimpf und Hohne?

Wachtmeister.

Da will ich euch dienen. Es ist nicht ganz ohne!
Der Feldherr ist wundersam geboren,
Besonders hat er gar kitzlichte Ohren.

Trumpeter and both Chasseurs
(closing on him).

Silence! Or death your tongue shall silence now!

Croats (interfering).

Stop here, your Rev'rence! Please, don't be afraid!
But tell us all the Scripture‑truths you've said.

Capuchin Friar (speaking louder and louder).

Such a Nebuchadnezzar, full of pride, —
Archfiend and sullen Heretic beside! —
Assumes the noble name of *Wallenstein*
Sooth — he's the pond'rous stone — *the waller's* *) *tine*, —
That rolls like Sisyphus's down again
To be our stumbling block and lasting bane.
No peace in land, while rules this *Friedeland*,
Will be, nor from intrigues be *free'd the land!*

(*Whilst uttering these last words, which he spouts forth at the top of his
voice, he gradually retreats, the Croats warding off the other Soldiers.*)

Scene IX.

The above without the Capuchin Friar.

First Chasseur (to Serjeant‑Major).

Say! what means he about this chanticleer,
Whose crowing our great Captain cannot hear?
Was it not said in simple chaff and scorn?

Serjeant‑Major.

Ah! 't is not quite a fiction — I'll be sworn!
Of marv'llous nature born, our Chief appears
To have most wonderful and ticklish ears;

---

*) Waller's tine — *the stone‑wall builder's distress.* The
word 'tine' *is used by Spencer for trouble, distress, vide John‑
son's Dictionary.* Waller — *a builder of stone‑walls without mortar,
as found in Derbyshire, and other parts of England.*

Kann die Katze nicht hören mauen,
Und wenn der Hahn kräht, so macht's ihm Grauen.

Erster Jäger.
Das hat er mit dem Löwen gemein.

Wachtmeister.
Muß alles mausstill um ihn sein.
Den Befehl haben alle Wachen,
Denn er denkt gar zu tiefe Sachen.

Stimmen (im Zelt; Auflauf).
Greift ihn, den Schelm! Schlagt zu! Schlagt zu!

Des Bauern Stimme.
Hilfe! Barmherzigkeit!

Andere Stimmen.
Friede! Ruh!

Erster Jäger.
Hol mich der Teufel! Da setzt's Hiebe.

Zweiter Jäger.
Da muß ich dabei sein! (Laufen ins Zelt.)

Marketenderin (kommt heraus).
Schelmen und Diebe!

Trompeter.
Frau Wirthin, was setzt euch so in Eifer?

Marketenderin.
Der Lump! der Spitzbub! der Straßenläufer!
Das muß mir in meinem Zelt passieren!
Es beschimpft mich bei allen Herrn Officieren.

Wachtmeister.
Bäschen, was gibt's denn?

Marketenderin.
Was wird's geben?

The mewing of the cat he cannot hear,
But crowing of the cock thrills him with fear.

First Chasseur.
That sense is also in the lion found.

Serjeant-Major.
Still as a mouse must all be kept around.
This order 's giv'n to sentries at his gates;
For deeply o'er all things he ruminates.

Voices in the Tent (uprour and riot).
Seize him, the Scoundrel! Knock him down or kill —

The Peasant's voice (behind the scenes).
Oh! help! Have mercy on me!

Other voices.
Peace! Be still!

First Chasseur.
The Dev'l take me! Blows fall like autumn-leaves.

Second Chasseur.
I must go in for it! (running into the Tent).

Cantinière (coming out of it).
All rogues and thieves!

Trumpeter.
Pray, mistress! What puts you in such a huff?

Cantinière.
Of that raff, cheat, and rogue I've had enough!
That such a scene should in my tent take place!
With Officers it brings me in disgrace.

Serjeant-Major.
Well, coz, what is 't?

Cantinière.
Why, what 's the matter now!

Da erwischten sie einen Bauer eben,
Der falsche Würfel thät bei sich haben.

Trompeter.
Sie bringen ihn hier mit seinem Knaben.

Zehnter Auftritt.
Soldaten bringen den Bauer geschleppt.

Erster Jäger.
Der muß baumeln!

Scharfschützen und Dragoner.
Zum Profoß! zum Profoß!

Wachtmeister.
Das Mandat ist noch kürzlich ausgegangen.

Marketenderin.
In einer Stunde seh' ich ihn hangen!

Wachtmeister.
Böses Gewerbe bringt bösen Lohn.

Erster Arkebusier (zum andern).
Das kommt von der Desperation.
Denn seht, erst thut man sie ruinieren,
Das heißt sie zum Stehlen selbst verführen.

Trompeter.
Was? Was? Ihr red't ihm das Wort noch gar?
Dem Hunde! Thut euch der Teufel plagen?

Erster Arkebusier.
Der Bauer ist auch ein Mensch — so zu sagen.

Erster Jäger (zum Trompeter).
Laß sie gehen! sind Tiefenbacher,

They have just caught a clod — for that 's the row —
Who with false dice their coin had freely won.

Trumpeter.
They bring him here together with his son.

Scene X.

Soldiers (dragging in the Peasant).

First Chasseur.
He must be hang'd!

Riflemen and Dragoons.
To the Provost off straight!

Serjeant-Major.
The law just publish'd now ordains this fate.

Cantinière.
I'll see him in an hour then hanging fast!

Sergeant-Major.
Bad bus'ness ever brings bad gain at last!

First Arquebusier (to the others).
This only can from desperation spring.
First these poor creatures you to ruin bring,
And then to stealing you their minds seduce.

Trumpeter.
What! what! You speak in his behalf? The Deuce
Take you for thus defending such a cur.

First Arquebusier.
The peasant is a man — so I infer.

First Chasseur (to Trumpeter).
From Tiefenbach's they are — so let them go!

Gevatter Schneider und Handschuhmacher!
Lagen in Garnison zu Brieg,
Wissen viel, was der Brauch ist im Krieg.

Eilfter Auftritt.

Vorige. Kürassiere.

Erster Kürassier.

Friede! Was gibt's mit dem Bauer da?

Erster Scharfschütz.

's ist ein Schelm, hat im Spiel betrogen!

Erster Kürassier.

Hat er dich betrogen etwa?

Erster Scharfschütz.

Ja, und hat mich rein ausgezogen.

Erster Kürassier.

Wie? Du bist ein Friedländischer Mann,
Kannst dich so wegwerfen und blamieren,
Mit einem Bauer dein Glück probieren?
Der laufe, was er laufen kann.

(Bauer entwischt, die Andern treten zusammen.)

Erster Arkebusier.

Der macht kurze Arbeit, ist resolut,
Das ist mit solchem Volke gut.
Was ist's für einer? Es ist kein Böhm.

Marketenderin.

's ist ein Wallon! Respect vor dem!
Von des Pappenheims Kürassieren.

Tailors and glovers they're by trade, I know!
In garrison at Brieg they lay there long;
Much know they customs that to war belong!

Scene XI.

The above, Cuirassiers.

First Cuirassier.
Peace! What's the row with that clodhopper? Say!

First Rifleman.
A sharper, who has cheated us at play.

First Cuirassier.
Have you then e'er been cheated by that chap?

First Rifleman.
He clean'd me out, and left me not a rap.

First Cuirassier.
How so? Can you then — one of "Friedland's own" —
Debase yourself, and shew such *mauvais ton*,
As with a clod to try your chance at play?
Off! lout! and run with all your might away!
(The Peasant escapes; the others throng together.)

First Arquebusier.
Short work he makes of it — that's resolute;
With people, such as they, one must be cute.
Whence comes he? No Bohemian, I suspect!

Cantinière.
He's a Walloon! Give him then all respect!
He's one of Pappenheim's own Cuirassiers.

Erster Dragoner (tritt dazu).

Der Piccolomini, der junge, thut sie jetzt führen.
Den haben sie sich aus eigner Macht
Zum Oberst gesetzt in der Lützner Schlacht,
Als Pappenheim umgekommen.

Erster Arkebusier.

Haben sie sich so was 'rausgenommen?

Erster Dragoner.

Dies Regiment hat was voraus.
Es war immer voran bei jedem Strauß.
Darf auch seine eigene Justiz ausüben,
Und der Friedländer thut's besonders lieben.

Erster Kürassier (zum andern).

Ist's auch gewiß? Wer bracht' es aus?

Zweiter Kürassier.

Ich hab's aus des Obersts eigenem Munde.

Erster Kürassier.

Was Teufel! Wir sind nicht ihre Hunde.

Erster Jäger.

Was haben die da? Sind voller Gift.

Zweiter Jäger.

Ist's was, ihr Herrn, das uns mitbetrifft?

Erster Kürassier.

Es hat sich keiner drüber zu freuen.
(Soldaten treten herzu.)
Sie wollen uns in die Niederland' leihen;
Kürassiere, Jäger, reitende Schützen,
Sollen achttausend Mann aufsitzen.

Marketenderin.

Was? Was? Da sollen wir wieder wandern?
Bin erst seit gestern zurück aus Flandern.

First Dragoon (joining them).

At whose head Piccolomini careers —
The younger — whom they chose of their free will,
When Pappenheim in death was bleeding still
At Lützen, as their Colonel Commandant.

First Arquebusier.

Durst they act so rash and intolerant?

First Dragoon.

This Corps doth sundry privileges claim.
Foremost in ev'ry fight it earn'd its fame,
Holds the *"jus gladii"* and its own laws,
And wins our Friedland's love and just applause.

First Cuirassier (to the Second).

Is't so? Who blurted it about to all?

Second Cuirassier.

Ay! from our Colonel's lips I heard it fall.

First Cuirassier.

The Deuce take us! We're not their driv'lling hounds.

First Chasseur.

You're full of venom; what's the matter? 'Zounds!

Second Chasseur.

Is it a matter that concerns us near?

First Cuirassier.

Sooth! — there's no need of much rejoicing here!
(The Soldiers draw round him.)
They want to lend us to the Netherlands;
Rifles, Chasseurs, and Cuirassiers — all hands
They want — Eight Thousand Men must mount their steeds.

Cantinière.

Ah! What! to march again, is't all one needs?
From Flanders only yesterday I came.

5 *

Zweiter Kürassier (zu den Dragonern).

Ihr Buttlerischen, sollt auch mitreiten.

Erster Kürassier.

Und absonderlich wir Wallonen.

Marketenderin.

Ei, das sind ja die allerbesten Schwadronen!

Erster Kürassier.

Den aus Mailand sollen wir hinbegleiten.

Erster Jäger.

Den Infanten! Das ist ja kurios!

Zweiter Jäger.

Den Pfaffen! Da geht der Teufel los.

Erster Kürassier.

Wir sollen von dem Friedländer lassen,
Der den Soldaten so nobel hält,
Mit dem Spanier ziehen zu Feld,
Dem Knauser, den wir von Herzen hassen?
Nein, das geht nicht! Wir laufen fort.

Trompeter.

Was zum Henker! sollen wir dort?
Dem Kaiser verkauften wir unser Blut
Und nicht dem hispanischen rothen Hut.

Zweiter Jäger.

Auf des Friedländers Wort und Credit allein
Haben wir Reitersdienst genommen;
Wär's nicht aus Lieb' für den Wallenstein,
Der Ferdinand hätt' uns nimmer bekommen.

Erster Dragoner.

Thät uns der Friedländer nicht formieren?
Seine Fortuna soll uns führen.

Second Cuirassier (to the Dragoons).

Butler's Dragoons to march they also name.

First Cuirassier.

And us, Walloons; especially they say.

Cantinière.

No doubt! they're the best Squadrons of the day!

First Cuirassier.

The Milanese we're to escort in state.

First Chasseur.

Th' Infanta! — That's an odd and curious fate!

Second Chasseur.

That Priest! — Then hell's broke loose o'er all the land!

First Cuirassier.

Shall we then leave our Friedland's own command —
Who nobly grants his Troops what wealth can yield -
And with priest-ridden Spaniards take the field
For that curmudgeon, whom we curse all day?
No! that won't do! We 'll sooner run away!

Trumpeter.

Why! what the Deuce, I ask, should we do there?
Our blood to Kaiser we have sold quite fair,
Not to that priest-like Spaniard's scarlet hat.

Second Chasseur.

On Friedland's word and great renown — for that
Alone — we 'listed in a mounted Corps;
Save for the love, to Wallenstein we bore,
Ne'er would have held us Kaiser Ferdinand.

First Dragoon.

Were we not train'd by Friedland's skilful hand?
Let us then follow his bright destiny!

Wachtmeister.

Laßt euch bedeuten, hört mich an.
Mit dem Gered' da ist's nicht gethan.
Ich sehe weiter, als ihr alle,
Dahinter steckt eine böse Falle.

Erster Jäger.

Hört das Befehlbuch! Stille doch!

Wachtmeister.

Bäschen Gustel, füllt mir erst noch
Ein Gläschen Melnecker für den Magen,
Alsdann will ich euch meine Gedanken sagen.

Marketenderin (ihm einschenkend).

Hier, Herr Wachtmeister! Er macht mir Schrecken.
Es wird doch nichts Böses dahinter stecken!

Wachtmeister.

Seht, ihr Herrn, das ist all recht gut,
Daß jeder das Nächste bedenken thut;
Aber, pflegt der Feldherr zu sagen,
Man muß immer das Ganze überschlagen.
Wir nennen uns alle des Friedländers Truppen.
Der Bürger, er nimmt uns ins Quartier
Und pflegt uns und kocht uns warme Suppen.
Der Bauer muß den Gaul und den Stier
Vorspannen an unsre Bagagewagen,
Vergebens wird er sich drüber beklagen.
Läßt sich ein Gefreiter mit sieben Mann
In einem Dorfe von weitem spüren,
Er ist die Obrigkeit drinn und kann
Nach Lust drinn walten und commandieren.
Zum Henker! sie mögen uns alle nicht,
Und sähen des Teufels sein Angesicht

Serjeant - Major.

Be set to rights, and lend an ear to me.
Talking is vain, it will not help us here.
Farther than you I see and quite as clear;
In distance looms a pitfall foul, though dim. –

First Chasseur.

Now hear the Order - Book, and list to him!

Serjeant - Major.

Come first of all — fill me, my Gussy dear!
A glass of Melneck wine my soul to cheer!
And then I will my thoughts to you disclose.

Cantinière (pouring out a glass of wine).

Here! Serjeant - Major, drink! God only knows,
How I'm alarm'd by your mysterious mien;
Forebodes it not some ill that lurks unseen?

Serjeant - Major.

Now, Comrades, look! 'Tis good and right I find,
That each, what happens next, should bear in mind;
But, as our Chief was always wont to say,
The whole of ev'ry thing one ought to weigh.
Friedland's own troops we all assume to be;
Householders grant for billets quarters free,
Attend on us, and cook our daily meals;
With horse and oxen, too, the Peasant feels
In duty bound our Baggage to convey;
This custom e'er in vain would he gainsay!
Should a Lance-Corp'ral's Party near in sight
Of rustic village and therein alight;
Authority he will assume strait - way,
And, as he likes, can there both rule and sway.
By Jove! Tow'rds all of us no love they bear;
The Devil's face they would much sooner care

Weit lieber, als unsre gelben Kolletter.
Warum schmeißen sie uns nicht aus dem Land? Potz Wetter!
Sind uns an Anzahl doch überlegen,
Führen den Knüttel, wie wir den Degen.
Warum dürfen wir ihrer lachen?
Weil wir einen furchtbaren Haufen ausmachen!

Erster Jäger.

Ja, ja, im Ganzen, da sitzt die Macht!
Der Friedländer hat das wohl erfahren,
Wie er dem Kaiser vor acht — neun Jahren
Die große Armee zusammenbracht.
Sie wollten erst nur von Zwölftausend hören:
Die, sagt' er, die kann ich nicht ernähren;
Aber ich will Sechzigtausend werben,
Die, weiß ich, werden nicht Hungers sterben.
Und so wurden wir Wallensteiner.

Wachtmeister.

Zum Exempel, da hack' mir einer
Von den fünf Fingern, die ich hab',
Hier an der Rechten den kleinen ab.
Habt ihr mir den Finger bloß genommen?
Nein, beim Kukuk, ich bin um die Hand gekommen!
's ist nur ein Stumpf und nichts mehr werth.
Ja, und diese achttausend Pferd,
Die man nach Flandern jetzt begehrt,
Sind von der Armee nur der kleine Finger.
Läßt man sie ziehn, ihr tröstet euch,
Wir seien um ein Fünftel nur geringer?
Prost Mahlzeit! da fällt das Ganze gleich.
Die Furcht ist weg, der Respect, die Scheu,

To see than our deep-yellow facings! — 'Zounds!
Why don't they oust us from their lands? Those Hounds!
For they outnumber us by all accord
And carry cudgels as we do the sword.
Why dare we laugh at them? — This comes to pass,
Because we form a formidable mass!

First Chasseur.

Yes — in united masses pòw'r will dwell!
The Friedland's warrior learnt that maxim well,
When he to Kaiser — eight years gone or nine —
Brought his great army forth — a sight so fine!
Twelve thousand Men were all they hop'd to need;
"That number," then quoth he, "I cannot feed!"
"But I will sixty thousand Men enrol;
From hunger, well I know, will die no soul."
And thus we Wallensteiners all became.

Serjeant-Major.

Suppose, for instance, one of you should maim
Me here by chopping off, whilst I'm alive,
My little finger from the other five
On my right-hand; pray, now what have you done?
Destroy'd a finger — other damage none?
By Jingo! I assert, I've lost my hand —
'T is a mere stump, that further work can't stand!
And so it is with this eight-thousand Horse,
Which they to Flanders want to send across;
Our army's little finger they are now;
If they march, you in consolation vow,
We only are a fifth in numbers less!
But then all union ceases — what a mess! —
All fear is gone, respect, too, and reserve;

Da schwillt dem Bauer der Kamm aufs neu,
Da schreiben sie uns in der Wiener Kanzlei
Den Quartier = und den Küchenzettel,
Und es ist wieder der alte Bettel.
Ja, und wie lang wird's stehen an,
So nehmen sie uns auch noch den Feldhauptmann —
Sie sind ihm am Hofe so nicht grün,
Nun, da fällt eben alles hin!
Wer hilft uns dann wohl zu unserm Geld?
Sorgt, daß man uns die Contracte hält?
Wer hat den Nachdruck und hat den Verstand,
Den schnellen Witz und die feste Hand,
Diese gestückelten Heeresmassen
Zusammen zu fügen und zu passen?
Zum Exempel — Dragoner — sprich:
Aus welchem Vaterland schreibst du dich?

Erster Dragoner.
Weit aus Hibernien her komm' ich.

Wachtmeister (zu den beiden Kürassieren).
Ihr, das weiß ich, seid ein Wallon;
Ihr ein Welscher. Man hört's am Ton.

Erster Kürassier.
Wer ich bin? ich hab's nie können erfahren:
Sie stahlen mich schon in jungen Jahren.

Wachtmeister.
Und du bist auch nicht aus der Näh?

Erster Arkebusier.
Ich bin von Buchau am Federsee.

Wachtmeister.
Und ihr, Nachbar?

The clod will crow again, you will observe;
From Vienna will War-Office-Clerks indite
Billets for quarters, rules for messing write,
And then us all to beggar's fare reduce.
How long will this endure before, the Deuce!
They'll take from us our Captain, too, away?
At Court no liking they for him display —
All falls to pieces! If the truth be told!
Who helps **us** then so nobly to our gold?
Sees that all contracts are most strictly held?
Who has the pow'r and strength of mind to weld
This mass diverse in one united whole,
And make them act, as one, in mind and soul?
Who has th'intelligence such laws to frame,
And then with iron hand maintain the same?
Now, for example, please, Dragoon, just say,
In what land did you first behold the day?

First Dragoon.

In Erin's bright-green isle; whence I came here.

Serjeant-Major (to the two Cuirassiers).

You are Walloon; I will on oath declare,
And you, Italian, as betrays your tongue.

First Cuirassier.

I ne'er could learn from what strange stock I'm sprung
Stolen in youth — from that my hist'ry dates.

Serjeant-Major.

And you, too, are not from the neighb'ring states?

First Arquebusier.

"Buchau am Feder-See" is my birth-place.

Serjeant-Major.

And your's?

Zweiter Arkebusier.

Aus der Schwyz.

Wachtmeister (zum zweiten Jäger).

Was für ein Landsmann bis du, Jäger?

Zweiter Jäger.

Hinter Wismar ist meiner Eltern Sitz.

Wachtmeister (auf den Trompeter zeigend).

Und der da und ich, wir sind aus Eger.
Nun! und wer merkt uns das nun an,
Daß wir aus Süden und aus Norden
Zusammen geschneit und geblasen worden?
Sehn wir nicht aus, wie aus einem Span?
Stehn wir nicht gegen den Feind geschlossen,
Recht wie zusammen geleimt und gegossen?
Greifen wir nicht, wie ein Mühlwerk, flink
In einander auf Wort und Wink?
Wer hat uns so zusammen geschmiedet,
Daß ihr uns nimmer unterschiedet?
Kein Andrer sonst, als der Wallenstein!

Erster Jäger.

Das fiel mir mein Lebtag nimmer ein,
Daß wir so gut zusammen passen;
Hab' mich immer nur gehen lassen.

Erster Küraffier.

Dem Wachtmeister muß ich Beifall geben.
Dem Kriegsstand kämen sie gern ans Leben;
Den Soldaten wollen sie niederhalten,
Daß sie alleine können walten.
's ist eine Verschwörung, ein Complott.

Second Arquebusier.

From Canton Schweitz my stock I trace.

Serjeant - Major (to the Second Chasseur).

Tell me, Chasseur, what countryman you are?

Second Chasseur.

My parents' acres lie beyond Wismar.

Serjeant - Major (pointing to the Trumpeter).

Both he and I in Eger first saw light.
Now! pray, who would remark. though keen of sight.
That we from South and North had been just so
Together blown and mass'd as drifted snow?
Pray! don't we look like chips from the same block?
And don't we stand together like a flock,
Compact and firm against our common foe?
To fit like cog - wheels in a mill, and so
To move by word or wink are we not taught?
Who has this engine then so perfect wrought.
That each adjusts a counterpart so fine?
No other than our noble Wallenstein!

First Chasseur.

That ne'er occurr'd to me in my life - time.
That we so well together fit and chime;
I heedless let the world roll round its days.

First Cuirassier.

In truth, I must the Serjeant - Major praise.
They fain would our profession ruin complete!
Soldiers they'd trample down beneath their feet;
That they alone despotic rule may hold.
A plot — conspiracy both vile and bold!

Marketenderin.

Eine Verschwörung? Du lieber Gott!
Da können die Herren ja nicht mehr zahlen.

Wachtmeister.

Freilich! Es wird alles bankerott.
Viele von den Hauptleuten und Generalen
Stellten aus ihren eignen Kassen
Die Regimenter, wollten sich sehen lassen,
Thäten sich angreifen über Vermögen,
Dachten, es bring' ihnen großen Segen.
Und die alle sind um ihr Geld,
Wenn das Haupt, wenn der Herzog fällt.

Marketenderin.

Ach, du mein Heiland! Das bringt mir Fluch!
Die halbe Armee steht in meinem Buch.
Der Graf Isolani, der böse Zahler,
Restiert mir allein noch zweihundert Thaler.

Erster Kürassier.

Was ist da zu machen, Kameraden?
Es ist nur eins, was uns retten kann:
Verbunden können sie uns nichts schaden;
Wir stehen alle für einen Mann.
Laßt sie schicken und ordenanzen,
Wir wollen uns fest in Böhmen pflanzen,
Wir geben nicht nach und marschieren nicht,
Der Soldat jetzt um seine Ehre ficht.

Zweiter Jäger.

Wir lassen uns nicht so im Land 'rum führen!
Sie sollen kommen und sollen's probieren!

Cantinière.

Conspiracy? Good God! What do you say?
My customers their reck'ning ne'er will pay.

Serjeant-Major.

Bankrupts we all shall soon become, 't is true!
For many Captains, and some Gen'rals, too,
Did give advances from their privy purse
To diff'rent Reg'ments, and largess disburse
Beyond their private means to make a show,
Thinking from this such blessings great would flow;
And they will lose, no doubt, their money all,
If our great Chief — th'Illustrious Duke — should fall.

Cantinière.

Oh! Lord save us! What ruin it brings! Odd Zooks!
For half the army stands upon my books.
Count Isolani   always slow to pay —
Two hundred dollars owes — all thrown away!

First Cuirassier.

What's to be done? Up, comrades, with one will!
One thing alone there is to save us still;
They cannot hurt us, if we all unite,
And use for One alone our banded might.
Let them send orders for our "Marching Route;"
But in Bohemia we will firm take root;
We will not yield — e'en one day's march to make, —
For now do soldiers fight for honour's sake.

Second Chasseur.

We won't be led about the country thus!
Let them come here and try it on with us!

Erster Arkebusier.

Liebe Herren, bedenkt's mit Fleiß,
's ist des Kaisers Will' und Geheiß.

Trompeter.

Werden uns viel um den Kaiser scheren.

Erster Arkebusier.

Laß Er mich das nicht zweimal hören.

Trompeter.

's ist aber doch so, wie ich gesagt.

Erster Jäger.

Ja, ja, ich hört's immer so erzählen,
Der Friedländer hab' hier allein zu befehlen.

Wachtmeister.

So ist's auch, das ist sein Beding und Pact.
Absolute Gewalt hat er, müßt ihr wissen,
Krieg zu führen und Frieden zu schließen,
Geld und Gut kann er confiscieren,
Kann henken lassen und pardonnieren,
Officiere kann er und Obersten machen,
Kurz, er hat alle die Ehrensachen.
Das hat er vom Kaiser eigenhändig.

Erster Arkebusier.

Der Herzog ist gewaltig und hochverständig;
Aber er bleibt doch, schlecht und recht,
Wie wir alle, des Kaisers Knecht.

Wachtmeister.

Nicht, wie wir alle! Das wißt ihr schlecht.
Er ist ein unmittelbarer und freier
Des Reiches Fürst, so gut wie der Bayer.
Sah ich's etwa nicht selbst mit an,
Als ich zu Brandeis die Wach' gethan,

First Arquebusier.

Good Sirs! bethink yourselves and have a care
The Kaiser's will and pleasure not to dare.

Trumpeter.

About the Kaiser we don't care a rush.

First Arquebusier.

Let me not hear that said again; so hush!

Trumpeter.

That't is as I have said, I will maintain.

First Chasseur.

Yes — I have always heard the same refrain;
That Friedland here alone command should hold.

Serjeant-Major.

'T is so — that is his stipulation bold.
Pow'r absolute he has — you know his mood —
War to declare as well as peace conclude;
He lands can confiscate and fines dispense;
A culprit hang, or pardon his offence;
All Officers and Colonels, too, install;
Short — he's the fountain-head of honours all;
This privilege did Kaiser self bestow.

First Arquebusier.

The Duke's great pow'r and wisdom we all know;
But he'll like one of us, for good or ill,
Remain the Kaiser's humble servant still.

Serjeant-Major.

No! not like us! You know that cannot be.
He is a Prince not mediatis'd, but free;
Just as Bavaria's Prince to th'Empire owes
Allegiance, so does he; — This each knows,
Who with me at Brandeis on sentry stood,

Wie ihm der Kaiser selbsten erlaubt,
Zu bedecken sein fürstlich Haupt?

Erster Arkebusier.

Das war für das Mecklenburger Land,
Das ihm der Kaiser versetzt als Pfand.

Erster Jäger (zum Wachtmeister).

Wie? In des Kaisers Gegenwart?
Das ist doch seltsam und sehr apart!

Wachtmeister (fährt in die Tasche).

Wollt ihr mein Wort nicht gelten lassen,
Sollt ihr's mit Händen greifen und fassen.
(Eine Münze zeigend.)
Weß ist das Bild und Gepräg?

Marketenderin.

Weif't her!

Ei, das ist ja ein Wallensteiner!

Wachtmeister.

Na! da habt ihr's, was wollt ihr mehr?
Ist er nicht Fürst so gut, als einer?
Schlägt er nicht Geld, wie der Ferdinand?
Hat er nicht eigenes Volk und Land?
Eine Durchlauchtigkeit läßt er sich nennen!
Drum muß er Soldaten halten können.

Erster Arkebusier.

Das disputiert ihm niemand nicht.
Wir aber stehn in des Kaisers Pflicht!
Und wer uns bezahlt, das ist der Kaiser.

Trompeter.

Das leugn' ich Ihm, sieht er, ins Angesicht.
Wer uns nicht zahlt, das ist der Kaiser!

How e'en the Kaiser in his presence would
Insist that he should wear his princely hat.

First Arquebusier.

For Mecklenburgher States the Prince did that,
Which as a mortgage did the Kaiser pledge.

First Chasseur (to the Serjeant-Major).

What? In the Kaiser's presence — you allege?
That's an occurrence rare — almost absurd!

Serjeant-Major (feels in his pocket).

Will you not then give credence to my word,
If in your hands you feel it once again?
(showing a piece of money).
Whose likeness does this bear?

Cantinière.

Come, show it then!
Ah! that's a Wallensteiner — I am sure!

Serjeant-Major.

What greater proof would you wish to procure?
Like other Princes rules he not his land?
Does he not coin as well as Ferdinand?
Possesses he not land, and subjects too?
To him as Highness subjects homage do!
Wherefore he soldiers must 'in force maintain.

First-Arquebusier.

That none disputes, so argue not in vain;
But we at Kaiser's feet our fealty lay;
'T is Kaiser self, who grants us all our pay.

Trumpeter.

That is a lie — I say it to your face.
The Kaiser 't is, who pays us not an ace!

6*

Hat man uns nicht seit vierzig Wochen
Die Löhnung immer umsonst versprochen?

Erster Arkebusier.

Ei, was! Das steht ja in guten Händen.

Erster Kürassier.

Fried' ihr Herrn! Wollt ihr mit Schlägen enden?
Ist denn darüber Zank und Zwist,
Ob der Kaiser unser Gebieter ist?
Eben drum, weil wir gern in Ehren
Seine tüchtigen Reiter wären,
Wollen wir nicht seine Heerde sein,
Wollen uns nicht von den Pfaffen und Schranzen
Herum lassen führen und verpflanzen.
Sagt selber! Kommt's nicht dem Herrn zu gut,
Wenn sein Kriegsvolk was auf sich hält thut?
Wer anders macht ihn, als seine Soldaten,
Zu dem großmächtigen Potentaten?
Verschafft und bewahrt ihm weit und breit
Das große Wort in der Christenheit?
Mögen sich die sein Joch aufladen,
Die mitessen von seinen Gnaden,
Die mit ihm tafeln im goldnen Zimmer.
Wir, wir haben von seinem Glanz und Schimmer
Nichts, als die Müh' und als die Schmerzen,
Und wofür wir uns halten in unserm Herzen.

Zweiter Jäger.

Alle großen Tyrannen und Kaiser
Hielten's so und waren viel weiser.
Alles Andre thäten sie hudeln und schänden,
Den Soldaten trugen sie auf den Händen.

Though promis'd forty weeks ago, each day
Does not in vain the soldier seek his pay?

First Arquebusier.

But in good hands 't is kept he always knows.

First Cuirassier.

Peace then, good Sirs! Or would you end in blows?
Why then d'ye quarrel and dispute on this —
Whether the Kaiser Lord and Master is?
Now just, because for honour and for fame
His good and trusty horsemen we became,
We all disclaim his common herd to be,
And then by priests and parasites to see
Us led about in foreign parts to dwell.
Say! won't it serve our Master just as well.
If soldiers their profession proud uphold?
Who then, except his soldiers true and bold.
Makes him the great and pow'rful Potentate
To rule o'er his immense and mighty state?
Who shapes and trumpets forth — both far and wide —
O'er Chistendom his word so shrill and clear?
Let them then bear the yoke and burden take.
Who of imperial favours need partake,
And in his gilded halls at table sit. '
From glare and glitter we get not a whit,
Nothing but pain and trouble — that's our part —
Save the proud feeling that buoys up our heart.

Second Chasseur.

Tyrants and Kaisers all, who had renown,
This maxim held and wisely handed down,
All men to plague, their happiness to marr,
But soldiers e'er to pet in peace and war.

Erster Kürassier.

Der Soldat muß sich können fühlen.
Wer's nicht edel und nobel treibt,
Lieber weit von dem Handwerk bleibt.
Soll ich frisch um mein Leben spielen,
Muß mir noch etwas gelten mehr.
Oder ich lasse mich eben schlachten
Wie der Kroat — und muß mich verachten.

Beide Jäger.

Ja, übers Leben noch geht die Ehr!

Erster Kürassier.

Das Schwert ist kein Spaten, kein Pflug,
Der damit ackern wollte, wäre nicht klug.
Es grünt uns kein Halm, es wächst keine Saat,
Ohne Heimath muß der Soldat
Auf dem Erdboden flüchtig schwärmen,
Darf sich an eignem Heerd nicht wärmen,
Er muß vorbei an der Städte Glanz,
An des Dörfleins lustigen, grünen Auen,
Die Traubenlese, den Erntekranz
Muß er wandernd von ferne schauen.
Sagt mir, was hat er an Gut und Werth,
Wenn der Soldat sich nicht selber ehrt?
Etwas muß er sein eigen nennen,
Oder der Mensch wird morden und brennen.

Erster Arkebusier.

Das weiß Gott, 'es ist ein elend Leben!

Erster Kürassier.

Möcht's doch nicht für ein andres geben.
Seht, ich bin weit in der Welt 'rum kommen,
Hab' alles in Erfahrung genommen.

First Cuirassier.

Soldiers feel what respect they must exact;
For he, who does not brave and gallant act.
Ought from his noble calling stay away.
If I so high a stake as life must play,
Then credit I must have for something more;
Or else I must be slaughter'd like a boor.
Or Croat, — and must then myself despise.

Both Chasseur.

Honour is more than life — 't is our great prize!

First Cuirassier.

The sword is neither ploughing - share nor spade,
To till broad acres none would say 't is made.
For us no grass grows green, nor ripens corn;
The soldier must pass by the home where born,
And rapid fly in swarms along the earth.
Nor stop to warm himself at his own hearth;
He must himself from all town-pleasures wean,
And calm pass by the merry village-green;
From far he must, while marching up and down,
Look on the vintage and the harvest-crown.
What estimation can he e'er expect,
If he be not imbued with self-respect?
To something, as his own, he must lay claim,
Or rapine, murder, — would be his life's aim.

First Arquebusier.

God knows, that 't is a wretched life indeed!

First Cuirassier.

Yet I no other sort of life would lead.
Look ye! I've nearly march'd the world around,
And in all matters form'd experience sound;

Hab' der hispanischen Monarchie
Gedient und der Republik Venedig
Und dem Königreich Napoli;
Aber das Glück war mir nirgends gnädig.
Hab' den Kaufmann gesehn und den Ritter
Und den Handwerksmann und den Jesuiter,
Und kein Rock hat mir unter allen
Wie mein eisernes Wamms gefallen.

Erster Arkebusier.

Ne! das kann ich eben nicht sagen.

Erster Kürassier.

Will einer in der Welt was erjagen,
Mag er sich rühren und mag sich plagen;
Will er zu hohen Ehren und Würden,
Bück' er sich unter die goldnen Bürden;
Will er genießen den Vatersegen,
Kinder und Enkelein um sich pflegen,
Treib' er ein ehrlich Gewerb' in Ruh.
Ich — ich hab' kein Gemüth dazu.
Frei will ich leben und also sterben,
Niemand berauben und niemand beerben
Und auf das Gehudel unter mir
Leicht wegschauen von meinem Thier.

Erster Jäger.

Bravo! just so ergeht es mir.

Erster Arkebusier.

Lustiger freilich mag sich's haben,
Ueber anderer Köpf' wegtraben.

Erster Kürassier.

Kamerad, die Zeiten sind schwer,
Das Schwert ist nicht bei der Wage mehr;

In truth, I've serv'd the Kingdom of old Spain
And Venice, too, — in her republic vein
And Naples — tyrant-monarchy — as well;
But nowhere could I lure good Fortune's spell;
The Merchant and the chiv'rous knight I've seen,
With Craftsman and with Jesuit, too, I've been;
But none of all the coats I've seen, I trow,
Excels the coat of steel, which I wear now!

First Arquebusier.

Not so! — in truth, I cannot say the same.

First Cuirassier.

Would in this world a man hunt out great game
He must bestir and plague himself anew;
Would he high rank and courtly honours sue,
Beneath the golden burden he must bend;
Would he enjoy a father's bliss to tend
His children, and on their's his love ingraft,
He must in peace pursue some honest craft —
I have no mood — to such I can't apply.
Free will I live, and free, too, I will die!
I'll rob no man; I'll seek inheritance
From none; but I'll cast down a cheery glance
Upon the mob beneath from my war-horse.

First Chasseur.

Ay! that's the way with me — just so of course!

First Arquebusier.

Yes! sooth it must be jollier sport and play
Careless o'er other's heads to trot away.

First Cuirassier.

Comrade! hard are the times and harder made;
In balance-scales the sword 's no longer weigh'd;

Aber so mag mir's keiner verdenken,
Daß ich mich lieber zum Schwert will lenken.
Kann ich im Krieg mich doch menschlich fassen,
Aber nicht auf mir trommeln lassen.

Erster Arkebusier.

Wer ist dran Schuld, als wir Soldaten,
Daß der Nährstand in Schimpf gerathen?
Der leidige Krieg und die Noth und Plag
In die sechzehn Jahr' schon währen mag.

Erster Kürassier.

Bruder, den lieben Gott da droben,
Es können ihn alle zugleich nicht loben.
Einer will die Sonn', die den andern beschwert;
Dieser will's trocken, was jener feucht begehrt;
Wo du nur die Noth siehst und die Plag',
Da scheint mir des Lebens heller Tag!
Geht's auf Kosten des Bürgers und Bauern,
Nun, wahrhaftig, sie werden mich dauern;
Aber ich kann's nicht ändern — seht,
's ist hier just, wie's beim Einhau'n geht;
Die Pferde schnauben und setzen an,
Liege, wer will, mitten in der Bahn,
Sei's mein Bruder, mein leiblicher Sohn,
Zerriss' mir die Seele sein Jammerton,
Ueber seinen Leib weg muß ich jagen,
Kann ihn nicht sachte bei Seite tragen.

Erster Jäger.

Ei, wer wird nach dem andern fragen!

Erster Kürassier.

Und weil sich's nun einmal so gemacht,
Daß das Glück dem Soldaten lacht,

Wherefore no one will blame to me award,
Because I've a strong leaning to the sword;
But yet in war I can humanely act
Without a drumming, too, or being sack'd.

First Arquebusier.

Who is to blame then but we soldiers all,
That in contempt the working class did fall?
The fatal war has lasted sixteen years,
Nor other fruit than want and mis'ry bears.

First Cuirassier.

Brother! To our all‑gracious Lord above
Not all at once can pray and show their love.
One greets the sun, of which will some complain;
One wants a drought, while others pray for rain;
So, where you only want and mis'ry see,
To me the brightest day in life may be.
E'en if 't were at the people's own expense,
Sooth, I deplore it much — in ev'ry sense
A sad misfortune — I can't change their plight;
Look! 't is just so as when engag'd in fight,
The horses snort and dash with headlong force;
Whome'er I meet athwart my rapid course —
Brother or son — his fate I can't condole
Although his cries of mercy pierce my soul,
Impetuous I must o'er his body ride;
I cannot gently carry him aside.

First Chasseur.

Who would about another stop to ask?

First Cuirassier.

Because things wear now such a pleasing mask.
When Fortune on the soldier deigns to smile,

Laßt's uns mit beiden Händen fassen,
Lang werden sie's uns nicht so treiben lassen.
Der Friede wird kommen über Nacht,
Der dem Wesen ein Ende macht;
Der Soldat zäumt ab, der Bauer spannt ein,
Eh' man's denkt, wird's wieder das Alte sein.
Jetzt sind wir noch beisammen im Land,
Wir haben's Heft noch in der Hand.
Lassen wir uns auseinander sprengen,
Werden sie uns den Brodkorb höher hängen.

Erster Jäger.

Nein, das darf nimmermehr geschehn!
Kommt, laßt uns alle für einen stehn!

Zweiter Jäger.

Ja, laßt uns Abrede nehmen, hört!

Erster Arkebusier.
(ein ledernes Beutelchen ziehend, zur Marketenderin.)

Gevatterin, was hab' ich verzehrt?

Marketenderin.

Ach, es ist nicht der Rede werth!

(Sie rechnen.)

Trompeter.

Ihr thut wohl, daß ihr weiter geht,
Verderbt uns doch nur die Societät.

(Arkebusiere gehen ab.)

Erster Kürassier.

Schad' um die Leut'! Sind sonst wackre Brüder.

Erster Jäger.

Aber das denkt, wie ein Seifensieder.

Zweiter Jäger.

Jetzt sind wir unter uns, laßt hören,
Wie wir den neuen Anschlag stören.

Let us with both hands grasp her for the while;
Long they won't let us lead a life so bright;
For peace may come quite sudden over night,
And put a stop to all our glorious life; —
Then soldiers will not harness for the strife,
But peasants will at once put to their teams;
Old customs will revive as quick as dreams.
Now here we're altogether in this land,
We all, too, hold our weapons still in hand.
But, if perchance we should asunder get,
Our bread-maund they will hang still higher yet.

First Chasseur.

No, no! — that never dare occur again!
Come, let us all to one e'er true remain!

Second Chasseur.

Yes, let us make a compact; silence, pray!

First Arquebusier
(to the Cantinière, drawing out his small leather-purse).

Sweet Hostess! tell me what am I to pay?

Cantinière.

'T is scarcely worth the while to talk about!

(They make out the reckoning.)

Trumpeter.

You do right well, that you're now turning out.
Our merry circle's spoilt just by such cads.

(Exeunt Arquebusiers.)

First Cuirassier.

Pity on those poor chaps; for they're brave lads!

First Chasseur.

Quite a soap-boiler's sentiment — that's clear.

Second Chasseur.

We are amongst ourselves, now let us hear,
How their last scheme we best can undermine.

Trompeter.

Was? Wir gehen eben nicht hin.

Erster Kürassier.

Nichts, ihr Herrn, gegen die Disciplin!
Jeder geht jetzt zu seinem Corps,
Trägt's den Kameraden vernünftig vor,
Daß sie's begreifen und einsehn lernen.
Wir dürfen uns nicht so weit entfernen.
Für meine Wallonen sag' ich gut.
So, wie ich, jeder denken thut.

Wachtmeister.

Terzkas Regimenter zu Roß und Fuß
Stimmen alle in diesen Schluß.

Zweiter Kürassier (stellt sich zum ersten).

Der Lombard sich nicht vom Wallonen trennt.

Erster Jäger.

Freiheit ist Jägers Element.

Zweiter Jäger.

Freiheit ist bei der Macht allein.
Ich leb' und sterb' bei dem Wallenstein.

Erster Scharfschütz.

Der Lothringer geht mit der großen Fluth,
Wo der leichte Sinn ist und lustiger Muth.

Dragoner.

Der Irländer folgt des Glückes Stern.

Zweiter Scharfschütz.

Der Tyroler dient nur dem Landesherrn.

Erster Kürassier.

Also laßt jedes Regiment
Ein Pro Memoriâ reinlich schreiben:
Daß wir zusammen wollen bleiben,

Trumpeter.

What? We won't go at all; for that's my line.

First Cuirassier.

Nothing, good Sirs! 'gainst discipline, I trow!
Let each to his own Corps depart then now,
And to his comrades with due care impart,
That they may understand and know by heart,
That we should not from here so distant move.
I swear that my Walloons will trusty prove,
Just as I think — and my opinion 's true —
Each man will think, and take from me the cue.

Serjeant-Major.

Count Tersky's Reg'ments will, both foot and horse,
Unanimous this bold resolve endorse!

Second Cuirassier (joining the First).

On union with Walloon the Lombard 's bent.

First Chasseur.

Freedom is e'er the Chasseur's element.

Second Chasseur.

With might alone true Freedom will combine;
Wherefore I live and die with Wallenstein.

First Rifleman.

Lorrainers will float with the strongest tide,
And join the careless and the jolliest side.

Dragoon.

The Irish always follow Fortune's wake.

Second Rifleman.

Tyrolese serve but for their Sov'reigns' sake.

First Cuirassier.

Therefore let ev'ry Reg'ment then unite
Distinct a "*Pro Memoriâ*" to write; —
That we e'er wish together to remain.

Das uns keine Gewalt, noch List
Von dem Friedländer weg soll treiben,
Der ein Soldatenvater ist.
Das reicht man in tiefer Devotion
Dem Piccolomi — ich meine den Sohn —
Der versteht sich auf solche Sachen,
Kann bei dem Friedländer alles machen,
Hat auch einen großen Stein im Bret
Bei des Kaisers und Königs Majestät.

Zweiter Jäger.

Kommt! Dabei bleibt's! Schlagt alle ein!
Piccolomini soll unser Sprecher sein.

Trompeter. Dragoner. Erster Jäger. Zweiter Kürassier. Scharfschützen (zugleich).

Piccolomini soll unser Sprecher sein.

(Wollen fort.)

Wachtmeister.

Erst noch ein Gläschen, Kameraden! (Trinkt.)
Des Piccolomini hohe Gnaden!

Marketenderin (bringt eine Flasche).

Das kommt nicht aufs Kerbholz. Ich geb' es gern.
Gute Verrichtung, meine Herrn!

Kürassier.

Der Wehrstand soll leben!

Beide Jäger.

Der Nährstand soll geben!

Dragoner und Scharfschütz.

Die Armee soll florieren!

Trompeter und Wachtmeister.

Und der Friedländer soll sie regieren!

That neither force nor artifice attain
The means to drive us from our Friedland's cause.
— The soldier's friend, who rules by love not laws –
This you present, in deep devotion done,
To Piccolomini — I mean the son —
Who is so conversant with such affairs;
With Friedland he gets all, whene'er he cares
To ask, and a great card he seems to be
With his Imperial Royal Majesty!

Second Chasseur.

Come! Stick to that and let us all agree!
Our speaker Piccolomini shall be!

Trumpeter. Dragoon. First Chasseur. Second
Cuirassier. Rifleman (altogether).

Our speaker Piccolomini shall be!

(all going away.)

Serjeant - Major.

Comrades! first let us drink a glass of wine   (drinking.)
"On Piccolomini may Fortune shine!"

Cantinière (bringing a flask).

That won't be chalk'd — I give it with good heart.
I wish you all success before we part!

Cuirassier.

Long may the Warrior's noble calling live!

Both Chasseurs.

Long may good food the Working - Classes give!

Dragoons and Riflemen.

Long may the Army its renown maintain!

Trumpeter and Serjeant - Major.

And long o'er it may Friedland glorious reign!

7

Zweiter Kürassier (singt).

Wohl auf, Kameraden, aufs Pferd, aufs Pferd,
　Ins Feld, in die Freiheit gezogen.
Im Felde, da ist der Mann noch was werth,
　Da wird das Herz noch gewogen.
Da tritt kein anderer für ihn ein,
Auf sich selber steht er da ganz allein.

(Die Soldaten aus dem Hintergrunde haben sich während des Gesangs her
beigezogen und machen den Chor.)

Chor.

Da tritt kein anderer für ihn ein,
Auf sich selber steht er da ganz allein.

Dragoner.

Aus der Welt die Freiheit verschwunden ist,
　Man sieht nur Herrn und Knechte;
Die Falschheit herrschet, die Hinterlist
　Bei dem feigen Menschengeschlechte.
Der dem Tod ins Angesicht schauen kann,
Der Soldat allein, ist der freie Mann.

Chor.

Der dem Tod ins Angesicht schauen kann,
Der Soldat allein, ist der freie Mann.

Erster Jäger.

Des Lebens Aengsten, er wirft sie weg,
　Hat nicht mehr zu fürchten, zu sorgen;
Er reitet dem Schicksal entgegen keck,
　Trifft's heute nicht, trifft es doch morgen,
Und trifft es morgen, so lasset uns heut
Noch schlürfen die Neige der köstlichen Zeit.

Second Cuirassier (sings).

Brave Comrades! now to horse! to horse!
On to the field — to freedom move!
For there a man feels no remorse,
And will his worth and courage prove;
There will no other take his place;
Alone each danger must he face.

(During the singing of this song the Soldiers have come forward from
the back-ground and joined them to form the Chorus.)

Chorus.

There will no other take his place
Alone each danger must he face.

Dragoon.

Out of the world is freedom flown,
Masters and slaves one only sees;
Falsehood prevails, and fraud alone
The coward human race will please.
The soldier, who looks calm on death
Inhales alone true freedom's breath.

Chorus.

The soldier, who looks calm on death,
Inhales alone true freedom's breath.

First Chasseur.

Life's troubles all he casts aside,
Then fears and cares will pass away;
Against his fate he'll boldly ride,
To-morrow — if 't is not to-day;
And if to-morrow, let us now
Cut off Time's forelock from his brow!

7*

Chor.

Und trifft es morgen, so lasset uns heut
Noch schlürfen die Neige der köstlichen Zeit.

(Die Gläser sind aufs neue gefüllt worden, sie stoßen an und trinken.)

Wachtmeister.

Von dem Himmel fällt ihm sein lustig Loos,
    Braucht's nicht mit Müh' zu erstreben;
Der Fröhner, der sucht in der Erde Schooß,
    Da meint er den Schatz zu erheben.
Er gräbt und schaufelt, so lang er lebt,
Und gräbt, bis er endlich sein Grab sich gräbt.

Chor.

Er gräbt und schaufelt, so lang er lebt,
Und gräbt, bis er endlich sein Grab sich gräbt.

Erster Jäger.

Der Reiter und sein geschwindes Roß,
    Sie sind gefürchtete Gäste;
Es flimmern die Lampen im Hochzeitschloß,
    Ungeladen kommt er zum Feste,
Er wirbt nicht lange, er zeiget nicht Gold,
Im Sturm erringt er den Minnesold.

Chor.

Er wirbt nicht lange, er zeiget nicht Gold,
Im Sturm erringt er den Minnesold.

Zweiter Kürassier.

Warum weint die Dirn' und zergrämet sich schier?
    Laß fahren dahin, laß fahren!
Er hat auf Erden kein bleibend Quartier,
    Kann treue Lieb nicht bewahren.
Das rasche Schicksal, es treibt ihn fort,
Seine Ruh' läßt er an keinem Ort.

Chorus.

And if to-morrow, let us now
Cut off Time's forelock from his brow.

(The glasses are here refilled, they hob-nob and drink.)

Serjeant-Major.

From heav'n descend good Fortune's freaks,
  They cost no toilsome weary days;
The serf, who in earth's bosom seeks,
  Hopes e'er some treasure to upraise.
He digs and spades, while life ebbs fast,
Digs till he digs his grave at last.

Chorus.

He digs and spades, while life ebbs fast,
Digs till he digs his grave at last.

First Chasseur.

Horseman and winged steed appal,
  For dreaded guests are they at least.
When lustres gleam in bridal Hall;
  Unask'd he comes to marriage-feast;
He woos not long, nor offers gold,
But swain's reward he seizes bold.

Chorus.

He woos not long, nor offers gold,
But swain's reward he seizes bold.

Second Cuirassier.

Why drowns the maid with tears her mirth
  And pines away? — Pray let him go!
Fix'd quarters he has not on earth,
  Wherefore true love he ne'er can know.
Fate drives him on in rapid pace;
Rest he ne'er finds in any place.

Chor.

Das rasche Schicksal, es treibt ihn fort,
Seine Ruh' läßt er an keinem Ort.

Erster Jäger

(faßt die zwei Nächsten an der Hand; die Uebrigen ahmen es nach; alle welche
gesprochen, bilden einen großen Halbkreis).

Drum frisch, Kameraden, den Rappen gezäumt,
Die Brust im Gefechte gelüftet!
Die Jugend brauset, das Leben schäumt,
Frisch auf! eh' der Geist noch verdüstet.
Und setzet ihr nicht das Leben ein,
Nie wird euch das Leben gewonnen sein.

Chor.

Und setzet ihr nicht das Leben ein,
Nie wird euch das Leben gewonnen sein.

(Der Vorhang fällt, ehe der Chor ganz ausgesungen.)

Chorus.

Fate drives him on in rapid pace;
Rest he ne'er finds in any place.

First Chasseur.

(He takes the two next to him by the hand — the others do the same.
All, who have sung or spoken, then form a half-circle.)

Then saddle, Comrades! quick your steeds!
  Uplift to combat bold your breast!
Youth champs and mid-life foams for deeds;
  Quick — ere the mind spirts out its zest.
If you won't stake your life anon,
Ne'er will a life for you be won!

Chorus.

If you won't stake your life anon,
Ne'er will a life for you be won!

(The Curtain drops before the Chorus is quite finished.)

Finis.